"You barge into my life and proceed to conduct some sort of military operation. And now you're going on like an interfering, dictatorial knave!"

Suddenly Lucas stopped and turned on his heels to face her. "Do you have an aversion to authority, Claudia? Is that what this is? You don't like being told what to do?"

The gray silken weave of his sartorial suit began to turn black as the rain seeped through his clothing. His overlong hair was already dripping and plastered to his smooth forehead and the high slash of his cheekbones. And the sight of him, wet and disheveled, flooded her with heat. Like this he was far more powerful and dangerous to her equilibrium. He looked gloriously untamed.

"No, actually I don't. Do you think it's right to force someone against their every wish? To blackmail in order to do your job?" Something dark flashed in his eyes but she was too far gone to care. "And because I dare to put up some sort of fight, you deem me as selfish and irresponsible. Do you have any feelings?"

"I am not paid to feel," he ground out, taking a step closer toward her.

"It's a good job, 'cos you'd be broke," she replied, taking a step back.

Lucas pinched the bridge of his nose with his thumb and forefinger. "You're the most provoking woman I have ever met."

All about the author...
Victoria Parker

VICTORIA PARKER's first love was a dashing, heroic fox named Robin Hood. Then came the powerful, suave Mr. Darcy, then Lady Chatterley's rugged lover...and the list goes on. Thinking she must be an unfaithful sort of girl, but ever the optimist, she relentlessly pursued her Mr. Literary Right and eventually found him lying between the cool, crisp sheets of a Harlequin romance. Her obsession was born.

If only real life was just as easy...

Alas, against the advice of her beloved English teacher to cultivate her writer's muse, she chased the corporate dream and acquired various uninspiring job titles *and* a flesh-and-blood hero before she surrendered to that persistent voice and penned her first Harlequin romance. It turns out creating havoc for feisty heroines and devilish heroes truly *is* the best job in the world.

Victoria now lives out her own happy-ever-after in the northeast of England with her alpha exec and their two children—a masterly charmer in the making and, apparently, the next Disney Princess. Believing sleep is highly overrated, she often writes until 3:00 a.m., ignores the housework (much to her husband's dismay) and still loves nothing more than getting cozy with a romance novel. In her spare time she enjoys dabbling with interior design, discovering far-flung destinations and getting into mischief with her rather wonderful extended family.

This is Victoria's stunning debut—
we hope you love it as much as we do!

Victoria Parker

PRINCESS IN THE IRON MASK

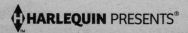

HARLEQUIN PRESENTS®

Recycling programs
for this product may
not exist in your area.

ISBN-13: 978-0-373-13158-7

PRINCESS IN THE IRON MASK

Copyright © 2013 by Victoria Parker

H HARLEQUIN®
™ www.Harlequin.com

Printed in U.S.A.

PRINCESS IN THE IRON MASK

Many thanks to my good friend Vicky. For all her patience and generosity in answering my questions about her son's fight against JDMS and how the rare adolescent skin condition has affected their lives. Together, they were a huge inspiration not only for this book, but for the way in which the power of love can protect and heal, inside and out.

For Nina and my family—thank you for sharing the smiles and hugging away the blues on my path to publication. Without your love and enduring support, reaching for the stars would still be light years away. I hope you enjoy my debut.

And finally, I dedicate this book to the amazingly talented Michelle Styles. You taught me to have faith in my writing voice and inspired me to believe. Without your unwavering conviction, Lucas and Claudia's love story would never have been told. So this, my dear friend, is for you...

CHAPTER ONE

'Lucas, my friend, I have a favour to ask of you.'

Favour?

Lucas Garcia had survived some of the worst conditions known to man, therefore a *favour* in his eyes involved hand grenades, automatic rifles or the calming of troubled waters on an international scale. What it unequivocally did *not* suggest was flying to London to retrieve a wayward snit of a girl, who disrespected the wishes of her father and showed no concern for her family or the country she'd been born to!

Anger blended with a tinge of discomfort in his gut as he took shelter beneath the green-striped awning of a coffee shop on Regent Square. Although summer approached, rain fell in heavy sheets, pooling at his designer-clad feet. Cold and inhospitable, the damp seeped through the wool of his Savile Row attire to lick at his skin.

'*Dios,* this city is miserable,' he muttered, scanning the wide glass entrance of ChemTech, London's foremost biomedical research centre, as he awaited the arrival of his current mission.

Claudia Thyssen.

'*Bring her home, Lucas. Only you can succeed where others have failed.'*

He was honoured by such high regard, and during his three years as Head of National Security for Arunthia he *had* successfully executed every order without question, standing by his moral code to honour, protect and obey. But this…

'I write. I appeal. Yet she ignores my every plea.'

Lucas flexed his neck to relieve the coil that had been tightening there ever since he'd left the office of his crowned employer two days ago.

What kind of person turned her back on her heritage, her birthright? Who would give up the luxurious warmth and beautiful lush landscape of Arunthia for a perilous city built of glass and thriving on iniquity?

As soon as the thought formed the answer came stumbling out of a traditional black London cab, weighed down with enough paperwork to make a significant dent in the Amazonian rainforest. Smothered in a long grey Mac, with her slender feet encased in nondescript black pumps, she blended into the dour backdrop seamlessly. Yet his avid gaze lingered on the wide belt cinching her small waist, enhancing the full curve of her breasts. Her dark hair was scraped back, gathered at her nape in a large lump, yet Lucas could almost feel it lustrously thick and heavy in his hands. Hideous spectacles covered a vast proportion of her oval face. But that didn't stop his imagination roaming with the possible colour of her eyes.

Princess Claudine Marysse Thyssen Verbault.

Hunched under the punishing thrash of rain, with the elegant sweep of her nape exposed, she seemed…vulnerable. Swallowing hard, he could almost taste her flurried panic as she grappled with her purse, fighting against the clock to be on time for a meeting he'd ensured would never take place.

Lucas ground his heels into the cement—*stand down, Garcia*—and stemmed the impulse to rush to her aid, erase her panicked expression. Instead he called upon years of training, focused on doing his job and concluded that her appearance was neither his care nor his concern.

Flipping back one charcoal cuff, he glanced at his Swiss platinum watch. With a jet on standby he'd estimated a four-hour turnaround, and frankly it was all the time he was willing to spare.

Taking one last look at the reluctant royal as she stormed

through a deluge of puddles, bedraggled and unkempt, Lucas stroked his jaw in contemplation.

Trained in warfare, and adept at finding the enemy's weak spot, he *should* be confident this assignment would be a stroll on the beach. After all, she was a biochemist—he'd captured mass murderers in half the time. Still…

'Oh, my God, no.' Claudia Thyssen glanced at the wall clock, swaying on her feet as she stood at the entrance to her lab. Her. Very. Empty. Lab. Instinctively she reached for the doorframe and gripped so hard a dull ache infected her wrist.

On any other day she would have been grateful for the isolation. So it was rather ironic that when she needed a room full of heavy pockets to fund her research the place was as deserted as an office on Christmas Day.

Her face crumpled under the sting of frustration burning her throat.

She was too late. Twenty minutes late, to be precise. Unable to avoid a visit to the children's ward at St Andrew's, where she'd been collating data for weeks, she hadn't banked on a monsoon and the entire city shuddering to a standstill.

It had taken her days to psyche herself up for this visit. *Long* days, considering she'd prepped through the night. Even her walk today came with a rattle, courtesy of a bottle and a half of stress-relieving tablets. But through it all she'd managed to convince herself that twenty minutes of spine-snapping social networking would be worth it.

Hot and wet, a single teardrop slipped down her cheek, and each framed article covering the walls—announcing her as a top biochemist in her field—blurred into insignificance. Because she was mere weeks away from a cure for JDMS— a childhood condition close to her heart—and her budget had careened into the red. Now fifteen months of development and testing would scream to a juddering halt. And the fault was hers alone.

Before the habitual thrash of self-loathing crippled her legs, she commanded her body to move and stumbled through the sterile white room, throwing the contents of her arms atop the stainless steel workbench. Shrugging out of her coat, she let the sodden material fall to the floor in a soft splat and collapsed onto one high-backed stool. Ripping the glasses from her face, she hurled them across the table and buried her head in ice-cold hands.

'Could this day get any worse?'

'Excuse me, miss…?'

Claudia bolted upright, swivelled, and nigh on toppled off her perch.

'Who are you?' Slamming a hand over her riotously thudding heart, she slid off the plastic seat and righted her footing before the mere sight of the man, almost filling the doorway, all but knocked her flat on her back. Hand uneasy, she brushed at her lab coat until the damp cotton fell past her knees in a comforting cloak. 'And how on earth did you get in here?'

She was surprised the floors hadn't shaken as he'd walked in. In fact it was quite possible they had. Because Claudia felt as if she were in the centre of a snowglobe, being shaken up and down by an almighty fist.

Of course it was just shock at the unexpected interruption, blending with the disastrous events of the morning. It had absolutely *nothing* to do with the drop-dead gorgeous specimen in front of her. Claudia had never been stirred by a man, let alone shaken.

Strikingly handsome, smothered in bronzed skin and topped with wavy dark hair, he stood well over six feet tall. Dressed to kill in a dark grey tailored suit and a white shirt with a large spread collar, he exuded indomitable strength and authority. But it was the silk crimson tie—such a stark contrast—wrapped around his throat and tied in a huge Windsor knot that screamed blatant self-assurance. Her stomach curled. Whether with fear or envy she couldn't be sure.

'Apologies for the intrusion. You left the door open when you came in just now,' he said, in a firm yet slightly accented drawl that shimmied down her spine, dusting over her sensitised flesh like the fluff of a dandelion blowing in the breeze.

Gooseflesh peppered her skin and she glanced down at her soggy lab coat, convinced her strange reaction was nothing more than the effect of rotten British weather.

With a deep, fortifying breath, she raised her gaze to meet his. Perfectly able to look a giraffe in the eye, she felt a frisson of heat burst through her veins at the mere act of looking up to a man. Yet the chilling disdain on his face told her she was wasting vital body heat and energy reserves.

Who on earth did he think he was? Coming into *her* lab and looking at her as if she'd ruined his day?

'You shouldn't be in here,' she said, her tone high, her equilibrium shot.

Claudia had not only ruined the day for thousands of children, she'd gambled with their entire future, their health and happiness. Unless she could think of a way to reschedule the meeting. Oh, God, why had they left so soon? Twenty minutes wasn't so long, and—

Her brain darted in three different directions. 'Wait a minute. Are you here for the budget meeting?'

Maybe he was one of the money men. Claudia could appeal to his better nature. If he had one. Because the customised perfection of his appearance couldn't entirely disguise a nature that surely bordered on the very edges of civilised.

His jaw ticked as he shook his head, the action popping her ballooning optimism.

'My name is Lucas Garcia,' he said, striding forward a pace and announcing his name as a gladiator entering the ring would: fiercely and exuding pride. With the face of a god— intense deep-set eyes the colour of midnight, high slashing cheekbones and an angular jaw—he seemed cast from the finest bronze. Beautiful, yet strangely cold.

A stinging shiver attacked her unsuspecting flesh and she wondered if there was a dry lab coat in the room next door. 'Well, Mr Garcia, I think you've lost your way.'

An arrogant smile tilted his mouth. 'I assure you, I lose nothing.'

Oh, she believed him. His mere presence pilfered the very air. She was also sure Lucas Garcia wouldn't have just lost the chance of three and half million pounds.

An unseen hand gripped her heart. What was the point of her life if she couldn't save others from what she'd gone through? Oh, she realised most of the children she met had families who cared for them, loved them—unlike Claudia, who'd been abandoned at twelve years old. But they still had to suffer the pain, the pity. The bewildering sense of shame. As with most childhood diseases, when adolescence gave way to adulthood the side effects waned. But she knew firsthand that was altogether too late to erase the emotional scars etched deep in the soul.

Eyes closing under the weight of fatigue, she inhaled deeply. She was so close to success she could taste musky victory on the tip of her tongue. Or was that his glorious woodsy scent? Good grief—she was losing it.

'I need to speak with you on a matter of urgency,' he said, the deep cadence of his voice ricocheting off the white-tiled walls.

God, that voice… 'Have we met before?' There was something vaguely familiar about him.

'No,' he said, standing with his feet slightly apart, hands behind his back, just inside the doorway.

Claudia suppressed an impulse to stand to attention. He was the most commanding man she'd ever seen. Almost military-like. Not that she had much to compare him to. One of the downfalls of self-imposed exile: she didn't get out much. The upside was that she rarely broke out in hives and she didn't get close to anyone. Claudia had no one and that was exactly how she liked it. No touching of her body mind or soul and there'd be no tears.

'I'm extremely busy, Mr Garcia,' she said, tugging at the cuffs of her coat, covering her wrists. 'If you don't mind…'

The words evaporated from her tongue as she caught the searing intensity in his blue eyes as he followed her every move, a frown creasing his brow.

Her stomach hollowed. *Stop fidgeting and he'll stop staring!* 'What exactly is it you want?'

'May I come in?' he asked, moving closer.

The word no was eclipsed from her mind as his body loomed impossibly larger. Within two seconds self-preservation kicked in and she edged her way around the desk to ensure a three-foot metal barricade. *Back off, handsome.*

Showing some degree of intelligence under all that ripped muscle, he paused mid stride, then devoured her face as if his eyes were starved. After he'd looked his fill their gazes caught…held. Claudia stared, mesmerised, as black pools swelled, virtually erasing the blue of his irises.

Pulse skyrocketing, the heavy beat echoed through her skull. After a few tense moments she blinked, trying to disconnect and sever the pull, unsure of what was happening. But no matter how hard she tried things just seemed to get worse: the temperature in the room soared and her spine melted into her pelvis under the scorching intensity.

'Why are you staring at me?' she whispered.

'You look like…' He blinked rapidly, his face morphing into a mixture of amazement and disgust as if he couldn't quite make up his mind what he was feeling or thinking.

The past slammed into her and she stumbled back a step. She'd seen that look on too many faces as they'd stared at her juvenile muscle-fatigued body, ravaged by skin rashes as unsightly as they were unfair. Yet the most destroying memory of all was the black-hearted response from her own flesh and blood.

Oh, God, why was she thinking about that now?

'What?' she asked, reaching behind her to pat the desk, searching for her glasses.

Lips twisting, almost cruel, he said, 'You look like your mother.'

Her hand stilled together with her heartbeat.

The glass door, the stark overhead lighting—all seemed to implode, raining shards of glass to perforate her carefully controlled, sanitised world.

Such a fool. So preoccupied with work. So pathetically enraptured by this man. She'd missed the signs staring her in the face.

His name. His deep, devastating voice. His fierce, powerful demeanour.

'My parents sent you,' Claudia breathed in a tremulous whisper.

No, no, *no.* She couldn't go back to Arunthia. Not now. Maybe never. It was a place she was only willing to visit in her imagination during moments of agonising loneliness. If only to reassure herself she was better off on her own.

'Yes,' he said, with a cool remoteness that made her shudder and remember all at once. For her childhood years had been made up of her parents' haughty detachment and hostile impatience.

It was their impatience that had condemned her, because Claudia had been an enigma no doctor could diagnose. Their detachment had sentenced her to extradition because she was an embarrassment—she'd been swept off to England, placed under the care of tutors, governesses and an army of paediatric specialists while her so-called loving parents forgot she'd ever existed.

They had betrayed her in the most unforgivable way.

The ache in her chest crawled up her throat and she squeezed her eyes shut.

It didn't take a brainiac to decipher their message. This man said it all. They wanted something and this time they were deadly serious. *Just fight, Claudia. You've done it before and you can do it again.*

She just wasn't entirely sure she had the strength.

Exhaustion pulsed through her weak leg muscles and her hand shot out to grip the edge of the desk as she begged her body to stand tall. *Come on, Claudia, fight. They don't need you. They didn't want the imperfect child you were. Don't give them the chance to hurt you again.*

Memories gushed like a riptide, flooding her psyche with such speed they threatened to break through the dam and obliterate her every defence.

Within the blink of an eye Claudia's day veered from bad to apocalyptic.

Lucas recognised shock when he saw it, and for the first time in his adult life the same emotion coursed through his veins, hot and unfathomable. While it blanched her exquisite flawless face, and widened her huge cat-like amber eyes, it completely severed his vocal cords from his brain.

Sans hideous spectacles, with wispy damp ebony curls framing her oval face, Claudia Thyssen was much like her mother. But where Marysse Verbault was strength personified, her daughter appeared almost…frail. The sight of her bending forward, her small hand pushing into her flat stomach, resurrected a dark tonnage of guilt that sat on his chest like an armoured tank.

Vulnerable. Undoubtedly timid. Traits he associated with the cold sweat of nightmares.

Yet his internal reaction to this woman was the complete opposite of chilling. The instant thrash of desire was so strong it knifed him in the gut.

She radiated supreme intellect, and Lucas would be the first to admit he preferred his women to be like uncomplicated candy. Covered from neck to calf in a frumpy lab coat, Claudia was more geek than glamour puss. So why did the mere sight of her raise his body temperature, thicken his blood?

Lucas frowned as his lethargic pulse slowed his every reaction and his mentally prepared speech drifted to the melamine floor in tatters.

Dios, why the bland exterior? She was the most beautiful

woman he had ever seen. Even the Queen's striking beauty paled in comparison to her second-born.

'Well, Mr Garcia,' she said, her voice firming together with her backbone, until she stood at her full height and he was almost bowled over by her stature and regal bearing. 'If my parents sent you, no doubt you have a message for me.' Her tone—now cold enough to reawaken the memory of frostbite—delivered the final blow. 'Consider it delivered.'

And if that wasn't a sharp swift kick out through the door, he didn't know what was.

What the…?

Realisation hit him square between the eyes, easing the tightness in his chest. Her façade was an illusion. An ingenious cloaking device to ensure she was hidden within a society who knew nothing of her real identity. For her resemblance to the Verbault line was astounding.

Grateful for the reminder of the real reason he was here, and of how beauty was only skin-deep, Lucas clenched his fists until spears of pain lanced up his forearms. Needing the dull ache winding through his body to regain control.

'You would be correct on the first count,' he said. 'Your parents have many things to say to you.' They were so anxious they had written countless letters over the last two months, begging for her return to Arunthia. Letters she had ignored. 'But this time, I assure you, their words will be spoken.'

Had she honestly thought she could ignore her family for ever? He'd been astounded to learn of her defiance. Such blatant disregard for her parents and the country of her birth.

The woman had no honour.

Treading lightly, as if flirting with a minefield, Lucas considered his next move. 'My apologies, Your Royal Highness.' No matter what he thought of her character she was above him in station, and he purposefully used her title, intent on her reaction. Her pale face remained impassive, which only served to prove his point. 'As I mentioned, my name is Lucas Garcia and I am the Head of National Security for Arunthia.'

'Congratulations. I'm very happy for you,' she drawled, raising one perfect dark brow.

Mesmerised, he watched the residual skittishness fade to be replaced with an emotion bordering on acerbity.

Twenty-four hours ago this was the woman he'd expected. *This* he could deal with.

'Your sentiment is appreciated,' he said, his silky tone forced for maximum impact.

Claudia focused those stunning eyes on him, her full mouth a moue as she sized him up. Lucas returned her glare, caught in an odd battle of wills, determined not to give an inch. It would be exceptionally easy to stand and look at her all day. If it were a power-play she desired he'd be a worthy opponent.

'How *are* my doting parents?' she asked overly sweetly, veering away, breaking the spell.

Before satisfaction could swell his gut, she began to shuffle around the table, shifting files from one place to another as she scoured the surface.

'King Henri and Queen Marysse wish to see you,' he said, somewhat distracted, his curiosity mounting as she searched the desk.

With a breathy little satisfied sigh that quite frankly belonged in the bedroom she reached over a paper mountain. Her lab coat moulded to her curvaceous bottom, the hem riding upward, giving Lucas a tantalising glimpse of sculpted ankles and sleek, toned calves. Swallowing hard, he whipped his gaze back up, just in time to see her pushing those huge ugly spectacles up her nose.

Swaying between the need to rip them back off or glue them in place, he cursed under his breath. *Dios,* he was not meant to feel anything. And the only thing he needed from *her* was to damn well comply.

'Well, I've no wish to see them,' she said.

Lucas kept his tone modulated, easy. 'That is unfortunate. They desire your hasty return to Arunthia. I have been commissioned to escort you home.'

She slammed her hands onto lush, rounded hips and her eyes fired darts full of ire. 'Mr Garcia, I'm not an express shipment. If it's haste you desire the door is directly behind you. Furthermore, if I wanted a vacation in Arunthia I'm quite capable of getting there myself. I don't require an escort.'

Lucas hitched a brow. He knew exactly what she required. A damn good—

'More importantly, I can't leave England right now.'

'Do you not wish to see your family? Reacquaint yourself with the country of your birth?' he asked, trying a little guilt on for size.

'Not particularly,' she replied, a hint of pink dusting her sculpted cheekbones.

Was she lying or embarrassed by her callous disregard? The notion began to appease him—until her arms fell listlessly to her sides and she bit down hard on her bottom lip. A drop of blood pooled on the plump surface and she sucked the flesh. Grimaced.

Miss Verbault was either into self-punishment or underneath her chosen façade lay an emotional maelstrom. Lucas decided to go on the first theory. If she had any conscience she would have returned home months ago.

'If they're that desperate to see me, why aren't they here?'

'Unfortunately they are incapacitated at present.'

'They usually *are* incapacitated, Mr Garcia,' she said, rubbing her brow with the tips of her fingers.

His head reared. 'Naturally. They do rule a small country. Something I'm sure is a time-consuming vocation.' What did she want? Weekly trips? How narrow-minded could one person be?

'Oh, I've noticed. For twenty-eight years, believe me, I've noticed,' she said, now rubbing harder, almost punishing. As very well she should.

Any other woman would be overjoyed to have even a small taste of the privileged life she rejected. To be royalty and live in pure luxury was, for most, an impossible dream. *Dios,* for some, placing food upon the table or returning to their loved ones at all was an impossible dream.

The woman was a conundrum. *You're not here to crack the code, Garcia. Just do your job and get the hell out.*

Lucas flexed his neck and battled on. He hadn't forged his way through the ranks by falling at the first hurdle or being a passive negotiator. Then again, he was adept at dealing with *men*. Not tall, striking, obstinate females.

Ordering his voice to remain civil, Lucas persisted. 'Regardless of their responsibilities, they look forward to your visit.'

A heavy sigh poured from her mouth. 'Oh, I'm sure. The question is, what do they want from me?'

A growl rumbled up his chest. 'They merely want to see their daughter.' He avoided the topic of an Anniversary Ball, celebrating her parents' fifty years of marriage, as had been suggested. Apparently she was uncomfortable at such gatherings. It was more likely she couldn't bear to leave her precious lab. Even Lucas could see it was the personal white fortress of an ice maiden.

'I'll arrange a conference call,' she said.

'In. Person.'

She snorted. Actually snorted. The most unladylike sound he'd ever heard. *Dios,* he'd met camels with more grace.

'I don't think so.' Turning back to the desk, she began to stack files. Then unstack them. Yanking at the cuffs of her lab coat every so often. His eyes narrowed on her small wrists. She was either cold or the habit was a nervous tic.

'Why now? Their timing is impeccable.'

'You *seem* to be an intelligent woman. Did you honestly think you could ignore your family for ever?' Could she not have mustered the decency to return one note from over half a dozen letters?

'Hoped would be more like it.' She swivelled on her heels to face him. 'I'm sorry, Mr Garcia, but your journey has been wasted. I've no intention of leaving here, with you or anyone.'

Crossing her arms tightly over her chest, she stood mutinous. His eyes dipped of their own accord, his pulse hitting one-fifty at the sight. Her pose had tightened the shapeless lab coat, offering him a hint of her rounded hip, cinching her small waist and enhancing the lush fullness of her breasts.

Blood hot as Arunthian lava seared through his veins.

'I'm afraid you have no choice,' he bit out, furious at his inappropriate physical reaction. 'Responsibility and duty outweigh personal desires.'

Claudia's luscious mouth dropped open and a fleeting image of those full lips pressing into his chest gave him momentary pause. His imagination flamed and he could practically feel her softness sliding against his strength. The heaviness of her breasts as he cupped the soft globes.

Primal lust hit with devastating impact. Sweat trickled down his spine. Torrid heat surged south. His groin pulsed once, twice, and hardened within seconds. Holy...

Lucas flexed his neck until he heard a soft click. What the hell was wrong with him? *Nothing that an hour with a woman wouldn't fix.* Any woman bar this one. Preferably a blonde. With blue eyes.

Dios, when was the last time he'd engaged in no-strings self-indulgence? Months? *Years?* No wonder he was in such a damn state. Working night and day had obviously begun to take its toll.

Claudia's sudden laughter crashed into his train of thought. A dark, hollow sound designed to chill the air.

'How wonderfully droll. I live in a free country, Mr Garcia, what are you going to do? Carry me out of here?' Laughter died on her tongue as her hand snaked up her chest to curl around her delicate throat.

The temptation to replace her hand with his made his palms itch. To caress or throttle—he'd yet to decide.

The air crackled with sweltry tension and Lucas raised one dark brow...

Claudia took a tentative step back. 'You wouldn't dare.'

No, he wouldn't, but she didn't know that. *Dios,* he was no animal. Although he'd witnessed many in his lifetime.

Suddenly his thoughts locked as his brain malfunctioned and an image flashed in his mind's eye. Nostrils flaring, he hauled air into his lungs and shut down the defect.

He searched for a retort. 'I would far rather you walked.'

She shook her head slowly. 'Not going to happen. Listen, just tell them I'll think about it, okay?'

Lucas smiled, although he imagined it was more of a smirk. What she asked of him was not only unthinkable but impossible. He was *not* going home empty-handed.

'I have to finish my work, Mr Garcia.'

Ah. He'd wondered how long it would take before she dropped the topic of her profession into the equation. The obvious chink in her armour.

'It's *very* important,' she said.

So was the country she belonged to. Lucas glanced around her workspace, troubled by the stark environment. After spending ten minutes under the harsh flood of lighting he already felt like a lab rat.

Control began to slip once more and he closed his eyes, breathed deeply...only to inhale a strange blend of clinical sanitation and elements of her work. Bleached cleanliness punched his gut, gripped and twisted with a hard fist. Sweat bubbled on his upper lip and he turned to pace, exorcising the demons. How could she stand being cooped in this cage? The violent need to escape pumped pure adrenaline through his system, and he clamped his jaw hard enough to crack a molar.

Shrugging off the discomfort, disgusted at his own weakness, he veered towards her. 'You may live in a free country but you were born to another and you have responsibilities to uphold. You will always have your work. But right now your family needs to take precedence. Three weeks at the most and then you may return. That is all they ask of you.'

'All they *ask?*' she flared. 'Why should I do *anything* for them?'

Lucas scrubbed at his nape, smacked with the need to butt his head against a brick wall. 'Your selfishness is astounding. Do you not feel one iota—?'

'I have responsibilities here, Mr Garcia. Petri dishes full of them,' she said, her arm outstretched, pointing to a wall where a bank of shelves held a legion of chemical equipment, jars and small plastic dishes of what looked like goop.

He raised a dark brow in her direction, only to be faced with one ink-smudged palm. The slight quiver of her long fingers betrayed her heightened state of anxiety.

'I don't expect *you* to understand what I do here,' she said waspishly and somewhat degradingly.

Lucas allowed the insult to slide, since he understood perfectly what her job entailed. If she thought him beneath her level of intelligence he was not only unperturbed—for it would be a cold day in hell before he valued the opinion of one so selfish and irresponsible—but his apparent ignorance would only serve to work in his favour later on. While he understood her motivations, her priorities were clearly misaligned.

'So,' she said, tearing her spectacles off her face, flaying him with amber fire. 'You can stop pacing like a caged animal, trying to figure out your next move. I've seen them all and I'm immune.'

Lucas clenched his teeth to avoid his jaw dropping to the floor. Incredible! She fought as a warrior. He'd never seen anything like it. Or felt anything like it. Because his entire body seethed with the need to haul her into his arms and kiss her pert, insolent mouth.

He scoured her face. Flawless apricot skin, huge distinctive amber eyes begging him for something he couldn't place. Understanding? Or to be left in peace?

Lucas could give her neither.

Failure was not in his vocabulary. He'd built his life, its very foundations, on honour, duty and protection. Not even an act of providence would steer him off his chosen path. Nor the most beautiful self-centred woman he'd ever laid eyes on.

Damage limitation was futile.

It was time to change tactics and up the pressure.

Because, come nightfall, Claudia *would* be returning to Arunthia.

CHAPTER TWO

IT MIGHT HAVE been nanny number four who'd told her not to play with fire, Claudia reflected as she took a tentative step back. But for the life of her she couldn't remember the woman who had screamed the warning *never* to provoke animals. Such a shame she hadn't listened and taken the same diligent approach to her safety as she had to her reading materials.

Standing no more than five feet away, Lucas locked his fierce blue eyes on her. Blatant intent slashed colour on his high chiselled cheekbones and her heart thumped against her ribcage. Without a doubt he would throw her over his shoulder and haul her out of here given half the chance.

Ignoring the ridiculous frisson of excitement *that* thought evoked, she focused on what was quickly becoming one of the most surreal days of her life.

Lucas, this dark, devastating brute, was by moral nature a carbon copy of her parents. Only thinking of their beloved country, of duty and responsibility. Uncaring of Claudia's desires or, more importantly, her needs.

Why should she do anything for them? What had they ever done for her, apart from abandoning her in a foreign country? Twelve years old and so sick she could barely walk. So unsightly they'd secreted her away. The loss of everything and everyone she'd ever known had soaked her pillow at night. So frightened. So very alone.

Throat swelling with the sting of past hurts, she swerved

back to the workbench and fumbled with the paper disarray for fear he'd see too much.

'I would like you to leave, Mr Garcia,' she said, the sheet in her hand quivering as violently as her voice. *Please just go.*

'You ask me the impossible, Your Royal Highness,' he replied in that delicious tone that licked at her senses like a hungry cat. Which only made her hate him even more.

She slapped the paper atop the stainless steel and braced her arms on the squared edge.

Trust her parents to send in the big guns. Lucas Garcia was proving to be as immovable as Big Ben, and she could hear the tick, tick of the clock. *Don't be ridiculous. They've sent for you before. You can get rid of this guy just as easily.*

Their last threat had been the abolition of her living funds. 'Go ahead,' she'd told them, and promptly moved out of her swanky three-bedroom apartment on the banks of the River Thames. The bluff had backfired spectacularly, because the vast space lay empty to this day. But she loved her kitsch one-bed studio because it was hers alone, flying the flag of her hard-won independence.

Stiffening her spine, she turned in time to see Lucas finger his over-long hair back from his forehead and her insides liquefied. Must be a chemical reaction linked to irate frustration.

'And please don't call me, Your Royal whatever. I know perfectly well what you're doing. Your tactics won't work with me.'

'Regardless of your preference, that *is* your title,' he said, his voice toughened like steel, brow etched with exasperation. 'When will you acknowledge the fact and behave accordingly?'

'*Behave?* I've always been the upstanding daughter, Mr Garcia. I work hard and, more importantly, I make no ripples that will reach Arunthian shores to embarrass or disgrace.' An implausible feat for Claudia, but he didn't need to know that.

The dark glower he fired her way said he was far from impressed.

'And I have two sisters,' she said, suppressing any girlhood nostalgia and focusing instead on the little she'd gleaned of them by searching their names on the internet. Just to see if they were well…happy. If the thousands of glamorous photographs and articles were anything to go by they were more than well. They were true royalty in every way. 'My parents don't need me.' Which was just as well because the mere notion of life at the palace, evermore in the public eye, made her skin crawl as if the venom of a scorpion pulsed through her veins.

'Good grief, I'm as far away from being a princess as you are from being Prince Charming!'

Lucas coughed around a closed fist, then uncurled his long fingers to stroke his jaw. 'I've noticed,' he said, searching her face as if looking for an answer to the question hovering in the air.

Why? Let him come to his own conclusions, she mused. Claudia owed him nothing.

In thinking mode his face almost softened, and for the first time she noticed beautiful long thick lashes surrounded eyes so dark, so intense, they glittered like sapphires.

'Then how would you like to be addressed?' he asked.

Claudia frowned, blinking over and over, scrolling through the past few minutes of conversation, slightly disturbed by his silky intonation.

'Just Claudia is fine,' she said warily.

'Very well, *Just Claudia.*'

Oh. My. Giddy. Aunt. Something hot and sultry splashed through her midsection. His accent thickened when he said her name. His full mouth formed a perfect O as if he'd kissed it past his lips: *Cllowtia.*

Kissed it past his lips?

She gave her head a quick shake. Twenty minutes in his company and she'd lost hundreds of brain cells, waxing poetical. This was what happened when a romance novel thrust itself into her hands during a spontaneous visit to the charity bookshop at St Andrews.

Claudia preferred to base her life on facts and scientific evidence.

And the fact was Lucas Garcia wouldn't give her a second glance if he passed her in the street. The idea of mutual attraction was laughable. She wasn't only socially inept but also the strangest-looking creature on earth. They were quite literally worlds apart. Or they would be as soon as she got rid of him.

From the way his long blunt fingers trailed down the lapel of his charcoal single-breasted jacket and deftly unpopped the button, it didn't look as if he felt the need to go any time soon.

Mid-exasperated sigh, the air locked in her throat as he rolled his broad shoulders, revealing a wide panel of crisp white shirt stretched taut over his rock-solid physique, and strolled over to where her qualifications hung on the wall, filling the white expanse.

'I understand you are a biochemist?'

Claudia's eyes narrowed on his fluid gait, lithe for a man of his stature, and her traitorous mind imagined all kinds. 'Mmm-hmm.' Oh, lovely—she couldn't even speak, her mouth was so dry.

'What exactly does your work involve?'

Was he really that interested? She gave a little huff. Of course he was interested. It was his job to be interested.

'At the moment I'm studying a childhood auto-immune disease and developing drugs to reduce the side-effects—along with a cure, of course.' Claudia just had to think of a child suffering from the same condition and her life made a strange kind of sense. She was here for a purpose. One that didn't include sitting around looking impossibly pretty, cutting ribbons at galas and chatting to foreign dignitaries.

Lucas paused before the largest frame. Her second Masters. 'You feel strongly about your work.' Reaching up, he straightened the gilt-framed plaque with tensile fingers and ran the tip of his index finger across the black lettering of her name.

The gesture was so unexpected, so intimate, it felt like a physical touch.

Without conscious thought she reached up and brushed her lips in a continuous circular motion, wondering what his too-large hands would feel like against her skin—rough and purposeful or seductively thrilling?

'The strength of my dedication is unimaginable, Mr Garcia,' she said softly, her hand plunging to her side.

Because suddenly, like the instant flare of a Bunsen, it occurred to her that he couldn't possibly understand her avoidance of going home. *Your selfishness is astounding.* In his opinion she was being awkward and highly unreasonable. Having no idea why the notion weighed so heavy on her heart, she wanted to explain. Would she see pity in his beautifully fierce gaze or scorn because she'd yet to overcome the lingering effects?

'That is quite understandable in the circumstances,' he said, with a cool sincerity that snuffed out her burning desire to elucidate.

Was he saying he already knew?

'This condition that you study?' he went on. 'JDMS?'

'Juvenile Dermatomyositis. I'm surprised you've heard of it. It's not a particularly common affliction.' Hence it was a constant fight to keep money rolling her way. Fingers of suspicion stroked her throat, curling like a noose around her neck. 'Did my parents tell you?'

'No.'

One word—sharp as a scalpel and just as ominous.

Claudia frowned. Was he deliberately being evasive?

Having reached the far corner, Lucas unclasped his hands and began to swivel on his heels. Before he made the full turn she braced her weight against the edge of the desk, clenched her fists, determined not to fidget and calling upon years of practice in the art of facial indifference.

Despite all her efforts her eyes still flared at the indomitable calculating expression on his face.

'Like you, I take my position seriously, Claudia. I would not be doing my job correctly if I stumbled into a situation without all the relevant facts to hand.'

Meaning he'd pulled her files. Not full medical—he wouldn't

have had the authority—so his information would be brief. 'So you understand my reasons?'

'I understand perfectly,' he said, his voice weighted with dark power.

A sinking sensation tugged at her limbs and she pushed her spine into the blunt edge of the bench.

'What I cannot comprehend is your reluctance to travel home. As far as I can tell, you are using your job as a convenient excuse. Luckily I had been forewarned of any possible obstacles.'

Panic pounded at her heart and Claudia bit her inner cheek to prevent an untimely sniping retort.

'With that in mind,' he continued, 'my first port of call this morning was with your manager. A Mr Ryan Tate.'

Her stomach lurched so violently her wheat-bran flakes threatened to reappear. But that didn't stop her brain firing synapses faster than the speed of light.

'That's how you gained access to this floor,' she whispered.

'Correct.'

'How dare you...?' Her voice cracked, failing her miserably. 'How dare you intrude on my life this way? What was discussed at this meeting?'

Lucas flexed his neck, his unease a palpable thing, but Claudia was far too busy stemming hysteria to take comfort from the sight.

'I enquired if you were free to take annual leave,' he said. 'The answer was yes.'

Oh...

'I asked him if there was anything standing in the way of your returning home immediately. The answer was yes. You have five days to secure additional funding before the work on your project is terminated.'

My...

'I questioned if there was anything I could do to relieve the time pressure and pave the way for your return home. The answer was yes.'

God.

She'd underestimated him. Badly.

Directing her voice to match the cool detachment in his face, she said, 'When you arrived I asked if you were here in connection with the budget meeting. While you didn't lie outright, you deliberately withheld facts which would have a profound effect on me. Why?'

'I had hoped we would come to an understanding without the need for—'

'Blackmail? Coercion?' she cried, her entire body trembling with panic and frustration.

Forget cool detachment. He was icily cruel—from his glacial blue stare to the hard line of his mouth.

'This is not personal, Claudia.'

'You've just made it personal, Lucas!' God, she had to control herself. Tears stung like tiny daggers but she swallowed every one even as they sliced at her throat. She refused to cry in front of this man.

For the first time his eyes flicked away from her. 'Do you or do you not require funding to complete your work?'

'If you've discussed this with Tate, then you already know I do.'

'Then consider it a favour for a favour,' he said amiably, his gaze returning, eyes narrowed on her face.

'A *favour*? What was the outcome of this meeting?' Stupid, stupid question—but she needed him to say the words before she gave up all hope.

'I informed Mr Tate that I would certainly consider providing the additional three point five million pounds of necessary funding if certain conditions were met. By you.'

'You… You…' The lab swirled before her eyes, gaining speed as if she were in the centre of a whirlwind. No. *No.* She was *not* going back. 'I'll find another way to get the money,' she said, desperation blurring her mind. *Don't be stupid, Claudia. You need the money. Take the money. You just asked yourself what your parents have ever done for you…let them do this.*

But at what cost? Her heart? Her hard-won independence and the little pride she had left? 'I will not be bought.'

The sides of his face pulsed as he clenched his jaw. 'Then I shall withdraw the offer. You can go to Ryan Tate and explain your actions. Neither of you will find such a large sum of money within the next few days. I guarantee it. So tell me,' he said, drawing it out, encompassing the room with one sweep of his hand, 'just how important *is* your work, Claudia?'

Stomach cramping, she forced her heels into the ground to stop her body from doubling over.

The man was heartless. He knew how important her research was to her. Knew of her personal connection. And still he was nigh on blackmailing her! No, he was using her weakness against her. Bizarrely, instead of hatred she felt utter disappointment. In both of them. Why in Lucas she had no idea. But in herself it was the heart-pumping, blood-fizzing desire that brought her such misery. So there ended her life lesson on physical attraction. She couldn't even trust her body to decipher the good from the bad. Then again, her body had let her down since she was ten years old.

'What exactly are these conditions?' she asked, proud of her unwavering voice.

'Three weeks' leave. Effective from nine this morning. Coupled with your return to Arunthia.'

Claudia shook her head slowly. 'Have you no conscience?'

Whether it was his words—spoken like an automaton, as if he were programmed—or his face—a picture of haughty detachment—her heart was torn wide open.

'I have a duty, Claudia. As do you. The choice is yours.'

CHAPTER THREE

DON'T YOU DARE crumble in front of this man, Claudia. Don't you dare.

An hour ago she'd prayed for a miracle and, as if the gods were playing tricks on her, they'd sent a warrior hell-bent on her destruction. The stronghold she kept on her emotions teetered precariously and her bones throbbed with the effort to stand tall.

Three weeks in exchange for three and a half million pounds.

Breathing in and out, slow and even, she locked her knees so tightly, a sharp pain shot up her thighs. But it was nothing compared to the blood dripping from her heart.

Lucas, the blackmailing beast, stood in the centre of the room, a dark lock of his hair falling over his brow in bad-boy disarray. Tall and gladiator-strong, he waited patiently—no doubt for a sign of her surrender. If she didn't loathe him so much she would melt at the sheer sight of him. He'd played her since the moment he'd arrived.

'Choice?' she said, and thank God her voice didn't falter. 'My so-called choice is either to follow you or lose my job, Mr Garcia. I'm fairly certain my refusal to comply with your conditions would land me in the unemployment line.' Oh, she could beg Ryan Tate to give her time to find the money elsewhere, but it would be a useless pursuit. There was a reason he was known as a hard-ass among her colleagues. Ryan Tate would question her sanity. Tell her to swallow her damn pride and think of the bigger picture. Don't look a gift horse in the mouth and all that. 'Then again, you knew that, *Lucas*, didn't you?' she said bitterly.

His throat convulsed and after a few seconds he relaxed his stance and rolled his broad shoulders. The fact that he didn't answer made her madder still.

'Who on earth do you think you are?' she said, her control slipping a notch. 'You went to Tate's office without even consulting me. Is this what I have to look forward to? A life of being coerced, controlled and dictated to?'

A light flashed in his intense stare before his face contorted with stunned incredulity. 'Since when does three weeks equate to a lifetime?'

It might seem a measly three weeks to him, but what would they demand after that? It didn't bear thinking about. 'Since you've given me a taste of the new regime!'

Lucas scrubbed his palm over his mouth, his chest heaving. 'Claudia,' he growled, his hand dropping into a large fist by his side, 'I am attempting to do my job, but your obdurate attitude leaves me with few options. Instead of focusing on *how* this happened, why not take some pleasure from what you will benefit from. Three and a half million pounds, to be precise.'

'But at what cost to *me*?' she asked. Then immediately bit her lip when the words echoed through the room.

'Three weeks of your time. It is nothing,' he said, with a savage slash of his hand.

A pitiful laugh broke through her thick throat. How wrong he was. Lucas had no idea of the personal price she'd pay. He was oblivious to her inner turmoil. But that didn't excuse his behaviour in her eyes. She was dedicated to *her* job, but did she go around blackmailing people? No.

'You speak of the strength of your dedication. Your work taking priority. Yet if that were true the money would make your decision in an instant. Or,' he continued, his mouth twisting, 'is it a case of you using your job as a convenient excuse?'

'No!' she cried.

Lucas's head reared at her outburst and she winced inwardly.

'No,' she tried again—softer, quieter. But it was altogether too late. The hitch to his brow told her so. And to some extent he was right.

When the effects of her illness had waned in her late teens her parents had visited once, maybe twice. Other times they'd sent messengers, and for years she'd declined everything from a short vacation to a simple dinner on her own turf, using her work as an excuse. Avoiding her own parents because they'd hurt her, betrayed her, cast her aside. When she'd needed them the most. If she took the money this day she would be giving them the power to destroy her all over again. *But you can keep your distance, Claudia. You're adept at doing just that.*

Three weeks of God knew what, in exchange for her funding.

Taking short ragged breaths to ease the pain in her lungs, she squeezed her eyes shut. In the space of two seconds her mind began its attack, assaulting her with a multitude of visions and images.

Arunthia—a world in which she'd been deemed unworthy and dispensable.

St Andrew's Hospital—where she could make a real difference. And—*oh, God*—the children trying to smile through the pain, the misery. If she lost her job work on their case would scream to a halt. Claudia was their advocate. They needed her. Could she ever look at them in the face again, knowing she could have helped if only she'd faced her past?

Pain cracked through her mind and her eyes pinged open. Lucas was staring, his eyes curiously hot and heavy, fixed on her mouth where she tore at her bottom lip. Gooseflesh pimpled every inch of her skin and she shuddered ferociously. Why did he have to stare at her so much? It was as unnerving as it was confusing. Made her want to reach up. Touch. Check her skin. Bury her face in her hands. Hide. But she couldn't. Wouldn't.

As if he'd caught himself, he scrubbed his hands over his

face and combed his glorious hair back from his brow with long blunt fingers. Heat flushed through her core and her breasts grew strangely heavy. She stroked her clavicle and felt the burn sear her palm. *Oh, great.* Her body wasn't complying with the new hate programme.

'Accompany me to Arunthia, Claudia,' he said, in a persuasive drawl that made her quiver. How was she meant to stay sane with a man who made her spontaneously combust? 'Despite what you think, I understand your desire to crack the elusive code of an illness that must've been difficult for you, but surely you can continue to work from home during your stay? With your family's support?'

Support? She almost choked. The very last thing she would ever get from her parents was support.

Lucas's gaze dropped to her hands and she realised she was tugging at her cuffs with the tips of her fingers. Again. Her stomach nose-dived to the floor. His eyes were like fidget-seeking missiles. She couldn't think straight around him. Instead of controlling her habits, which she usually managed to hide unerringly, she kept being distracted by *him*. Her attention constantly snagged on his long, powerful legs, his huge, masculine hands, his utterly contemptuous handsome-as-sin face. And no matter how hard she tried her traitorous mind kept imagining things—like those big hands touching her in all the places she felt warm and sensitive. Kissing her. Caressing her.

Heat slapped her cheeks. This had to stop!

Her life was crumbling before her eyes—her career, her life's work, slipping through her fingers like grains of salt—and all she could think about was being kissed. If that wasn't bad enough, she wanted the man who'd plotted her destruction to do it! She was seriously beginning to question her mental faculties.

Panic fired a shot of adrenaline down her spine, surging to every extremity. Her feet were the first to move and she swerved around the desk, walking towards the door with no forethought to her destination. But getting away from Lucas sounded like paradise.

Before she made it past he bolted forward, one hand out-stretched, reaching for her. 'Claudia. *Dios!* Stop. Do not walk away from me,' he growled. 'We are not done.'

Oh, God. She flinched, jerked backwards, and almost lost her footing. 'Oh…' Steely hands closed around her upper arms, steadying her, and she scrunched her eyes shut, unable to look at his face for fear of what she might see. Pity? Or, worse still, disgust?

Through two layers she could feel the heat of his palms, and the power of his grip fired a blaze of sorcery through her bloodstream. His breath tickled over her face and the scent of warm strong coffee wafted over her, making her crave a caffeine fix. As soon as she regained her balance his hands fell away and Claudia yearned for them to come back. Which was crazy for all kinds of reasons.

The noise of his throat clearing told her he'd moved back a pace or three, and Claudia opened one eye to check. Sure enough, he stood a few feet away, fists clenched, eyes raging with a storm. Darkness tainted his tone. 'Where are you going, Claudia?'

Somewhat safer, she opened her other eye and practically ran towards the door. 'I have to see Ryan Tate,' she murmured, grateful for the excuse that flashed into her brain.

'What?' His thunderous voice became a distant blur as she swerved into the corridor. She imagined him standing there, his gorgeous blue eyes glittering with ire, his fists balled to stop himself from wrapping them around her throat.

'Claudia, wait!' he hollered. 'We need to finish this. *Now!*'

'Go to hell, Lucas.'

She kept on walking, blinded by a mind-fog, and within minutes, oblivious as to how she descended three floors, she was standing in front of Ryan Tate's door, her fist hovering over the solid oak panel.

And then she saw it. The violent tremble in the hand poised

in front of her. Then she felt it. The pain searing up her legs, crippling her entire body. Quickly she turned and leaned against the wall before her knees surrendered. Tipping her head back, the beige paint a glorious pillow, she closed her eyes and swallowed hard.

Come on Claudia, get a grip, she mouthed silently. *Three weeks. Three and a half million pounds. Keep your distance. Stay away from Lucas the Devastating. You can do this.*

She just had to remain strong and self-reliant. Always self-reliant.

You don't get close, you don't get hurt. Breathe, Claudia, breathe.

Time ticked by, the trembling subsided, and the pain dulled to its usual ache. Finally able to stand tall, she inhaled a lung full of fortifying air, lifted her chin, raised her hand to knock once, twice...and walked through Ryan Tate's door.

'Claudia, my girl. Good news, aye?'

After years of honing her brave face, Claudia slipped behind her iron mask and smiled.

Sweat pierced the base of his spine as Lucas stalked the lab, focusing on breathing and formulating a new plan. As long as it involved getting out of this white box he'd be slightly mollified. Claudia might prefer her small hideaway, but he required vast open space to feel alive.

It hadn't escaped him that when the prickly Princess had been in the room he'd been less aware of the enclosure. *Probably because you only had eyes for her.* Lucas growled, satisfying himself that it was more a case of distraction.

Was she pleading with Tate to give her more time to find the money elsewhere? *Dios* she was the most awkward, feisty, self-centred, gorgeous woman he'd ever met.

She also despised him with a passion. The disgust in her eyes had almost floored him. Only a fool would have walked in here without the necessary weapons at his disposal. God knew he'd have preferred to reach some kind of compromise, but she was recklessly tenacious and ignoble at best.

Yet as soon as he'd revealed his tactical strategy his stomach had ached as if she'd punched him in the guts. How did she manage to unearth emotion from him? He knew she selfishly pursued her own agenda. Knew she'd given him no choice but to push her. It was bewildering. Unnerving. Inappropriate and unwelcome. For Lucas had buried his emotions twenty years ago, and that, he thought, hardening his heart, was the way they must stay.

Glancing down at his hands, he curled his fingers into his palms. He could still feel her; he'd swear it. Warm, toned, yet lusciously soft. And her scent—*Dios*, she smelled of summer. Warm notes of vanilla blossom and honey. Up close she was impossibly more beautiful, and as he'd held her he'd willed her to open her eyes. But the hate had still been there and she could not bear to look at him. Which was good—great, fantastic. Being likable was not in his job description. Getting her home, however, was.

'Why are you still here?'

His stomach flinched but he managed to become fixated on her fascinating collection of test tubes. It was her voice: snippily sexy beyond belief. Why a schoolmarm tone should flick his switch he'd never know. He'd never had a teacher in his life. Children from the slums were not afforded such privileges. No books, no paper nor pens to draw with. Only walls stained with tobacco, bloodied fists and a penknife beyond decay.

'A trip to hell was unappealing,' he replied thickly, knowingly. He'd been there plenty of times, after all. 'And, with the greatest will in the world, I cannot deliver a package I do not have in my possession.'

'Quite.'

Lucas swivelled on his heels in time to see her arch one dark brow, her eyes firing with newfound determination. And his chest seized with such force his lungs pinched with deprivation.

'You knew I'd come back, didn't you?' she asked.

'Let's just say I had faith you would come to your senses.' While she'd virtually admitted that she used her work as a shield to hide from her parents, he believed she loved her job. If he could admire her for anything, it was the strength of her dedication. What he struggled to comprehend was why she couldn't extend that devotion to her role in Arunthia. He wanted to ask her, to try to understand. But the longer he stood here, skirting quicksand, the more entrenched he became.

Pouting her luscious lips, she canted her head like an inquisitive meerkat. 'I can't work out whether you're extremely diplomatic or downright arrogant.'

'I shall leave that for you to decide.'

She walked farther into the room, snatched a pair of spectacles from a plastic tub on the bench, and pushed them up her pert nose. With steel in her spine, her head high in a model-type pose, Lucas was smacked with a vision: Claudia Verbault, strutting down a catwalk, wearing a ruffled blouse and a tweed skirt, sucking on a pencil. Seductively intellectual.

Blood pooled in his groin and his mouth turned as dry as Arunthian dirt. He had to drench his lips with moisture in order to speak.

'I have a jet on stand-by. We'll leave the country within two hours.' Lucas could have her home within five and his job would be done. In future he'd only have to see her at state functions. By then, having appeased his newfound sexual appetite, he'd be able to look at her without imagining her naked. For he knew her body would be sublime. Soft and pliable to his steel and strength, and tall enough to be the perfect fit.

'Rather presumptuous of you, isn't it?' she said.

Madre de Dios! Had he said that out loud? Lucas focused on her bent head as she slid the files lying on her desk into a large briefcase, one on top of the other.

He cleared his throat of pure want. 'What is?'

'To assume I'm leaving with you.'

The tightness in his neck drained down his spine. 'Apologies, *Just Claudia.*'

Her hand stilled, and from his sideways vantage point he watched one eyelid shutter while she inhaled deeply, her breasts rising with life, pinky rouge blooming up her cheeks.

Did he affect her? The notion sucker-punched him straight in the solar plexus.

Her gentle touch forgotten, she began to ram two or three more files into the case, pushing until the bag was fit to burst. Maybe she was imagining it was his head. Oh, he certainly affected her. With annoyance rather than sexual attraction. Instead of relief he felt ridiculously irked.

How typical that the one woman in the world he could never have was a nemesis he instinctively wanted to devour.

'So. What is your decision?' He already knew it, but if she wanted to put up the pretence of a fight he would humour her. For now.

Kid gloves were his current choice of weapon.

'I'm coming with you.'

His lips curved.

'But not today.'

They flattened faster than a bomb detonation site.

'What?'

'I need three days,' she said, adamant.

'Impossible.' He wouldn't last two days without assaulting her gorgeous mouth.

Lucas worked to his own schedule, but just the thought of spending time near that sensational body while his stomach churned with a noxious mixture of frustration and fury ratcheted his deadline up into the red zone.

'Delaying the inevitable is not only a foolhardy display of awkwardness on your part but a waste of time.'

'Not for me. I need to go back to my apartment and pack. I have a personal matter to attend to, and most of all I need time to think,' she said, tucking a wayward curl around the delicate shell of her ear.

'Think?' What did she need to think about? How many lab coats to pack? 'I have no time to spare.' Lucas blinked. Wait a minute… Personal matter? *Dios,* he'd never thought of that. And why did it make him feel like punching the wall?

'Tough. Find time. Because I'm not going anywhere today.' There it was again—that surge of heat when she used that sexy, stern voice.

And there *she* was, being selfish again. Why did he keep forgetting what kind of person she was? 'Claudia, I cannot stay in London. I have to work.'

'Oh, *really?*' she said, yanking the case off the table and almost toppling over as it fell to the floor with a thud. 'Well, now you know how I feel. I'm being dragged away from mine for three weeks. I'm sure you can afford to take three days.'

His nostrils flared. 'My terms—'

'Lucas,' she said, attempting to disguise her rude interruption with an untried honeyed tone that made his skin prickle, 'you will quickly come to realise I forget nothing. Your terms are—and I quote—three weeks' leave, effective from nine this morning. Coupled with my return to Arunthia. On no occasion did you state a day of departure.'

Dios! Lucas seethed. She was impossible. 'It is almost noon. You have eight hours.' Let it not be said that he couldn't compromise.

Arms crossed tight, her full breasts were pushed upwards to stretch the stiff cotton and she canted her hip in a sexy pose. The ten-bell alarm siren going off in his head almost rendered him deaf. Almost.

'Two days,' she bartered.

Lucas ground his jaw. 'Twenty-four hours. Final offer.' He was crazy. Certifiable. A day of Claudia would tip him over the edge of reason to plummet headlong into insanity. He did not negotiate. *Ever.* People obeyed him. Always.

She smiled. It might have been small and somewhat triumphant, but she actually smiled at him.

Lucas felt his eye twitch.

'Done,' she said, all smug sweetness.

God help him if she ever put her heart and soul into it. Because Lucas had an uneasy feeling it would be him that would be 'done'.

'Fine,' he snapped, his abnormal behaviour pushing his soaring anger levels from dangerous to critical.

He only prayed her apartment on the Thames had separate floors. Or at least a fifty-foot distance between bedrooms. Fighting with bloodthirsty night demons would be child's play in comparison to the blistering temptation that would be down the hall.

Lucas didn't look happy, Claudia mused. Waves of dark fury poured from his tight shoulders, much like the rain streaming in rivulets down the black bodywork of his Aston Martin Vanquish.

The engine of his Aston Martin Vanquish roared like a sleek panther as he revved his displeasure, and she wiggled on the cream cowhide in an attempt to cover her quivering reaction. She'd never thought of a car as arousing before. Well, she'd never thought of *anything* as arousing before. Today seemed to be a day for firsts. Even the heady smell of leather and damp clothing couldn't douse the warm, woodsy scent of Lucas lingering in the air.

With the exception of his barking request for her to enter her address into the sat nav, their drive to her apartment had been deadly silent. Now, parked at the kerb, she was desperate to be away from his fiercely primal aura. She was so tired she no longer had the strength to argue, and her legs throbbed so viciously she'd be lucky if she made it inside the building, let alone up the stairs.

'Erm…thanks for the lift, Mr Garcia. Unless the gods grace me with a reprieve, I'll see you tomorrow.' Without further ado, she yanked hard on the door handle. After a third *kerthunk,* she surrendered, directing her voice to be sweet. 'Could you open the door, *pleeease?*'

'Claudia,' he growled, nostrils flaring, his chest heaving with barely suppressed anger. Staring out of his window at the three-storey townhouse where she lived on the second floor, he twisted his long fingers around the dark wood steering wheel. Maybe he was imagining it was her neck. 'Have you ever once acknowledged who you *actually* are?'

'Who I am?' she asked wearily, not entirely sure what he was getting at and unable to summon the energy to care.

'Yes, Claudia,' he said slowly, as if speaking to a child. 'A member of the Arunthian Royal Family.'

Never. 'Not really. Can I go now?' She gave the handle another tug. *Kerthunk.* A long sigh poured from her lungs.

'How long have you lived in this…this place?' The way he said *place,* as if the word was rat poison on his tongue, was like taking a grater to her nerves. Without bothering to look out of the window, her mind's eye recalled a picture of the tired frontage of this Victorian townhouse on a less than stellar street. What was he getting into a funk about? *He* didn't have to live here.

Claudia bit her tongue and thumped her head off the rest. 'Oh, about eighteen months, I think.' She slept most nights in the lab—more for convenience than because of the emptiness that shrouded her body when she lay between cold damp sheets, she was sure—but she kept that titbit to herself.

Lucas continued to fume, steam blowing from his nose as he stared out of the front windscreen. 'You could've been abducted fifty times over,' he growled, and she lifted her head from the buttery soft leather to see him scrub his face with rough hands. 'Burgled, raped, assaulted,' he went on. 'What the *hell* were you thinking, Claudia?'

Pushing down on the froth of fury bubbling up her throat, she pursed her lips. He'd turned from blackmailer to overprotective bore!

'You're overreacting, Mr Garcia,' she said calmly. 'This is a decent area and I have an excellent alarm system. Anyway, who would look at…?' The words died on her tongue as she realised how pitiful she would sound if she said *me*. She knew she wasn't pretty, and she'd given up wishing she looked like one of her famed-for-their-beauty sisters long ago. Right now, faced with the most astoundingly handsome man she'd ever seen, she couldn't face the prospect of his sympathy or his averment.

'Who would look at *what?*'

For the first time in thirty minutes he turned to look at her. The intensity in his sapphire blues acted like a laser beam and, as if locked on target, she couldn't tear her gaze away.

Choosing her words carefully, she said, 'Who would look twice at a normal person? The problems start when people appear moneyed and pampered. I bring no attention to myself. No one would give me a second glance.'

Jaw dropping open, Lucas slowly shook his head incredulously. 'And what if your cover was blown?'

'I would move. Can I go now?'

'No. You *cannot* go now,' he said fiercely, and her hackles prickled. 'Why are you not living in the *security-enhanced* apartment on the Thames?'

Claudia stiffened and finally managed to wrench her gaze away. 'How do you know about—?' She held up her hand in a stop sign. 'Forget I said that. I needed to be closer to work.' A half-truth, but that was all he was getting. It was seriously unnerving to know someone had files detailing her life events. She imagined it read like a chronological disaster essay.

'You gave it up?' he asked, his brows almost hitting his hairline. 'To live *here?*'

For some reason she actually followed his finger, which unsurprisingly pointed to her flat. 'Yes,' she said simply.

'*Dios,* Claudia!' His hands lifted as if pleading for patience from the heavens. 'How can an intelligent woman be so unthinking?'

A ball of fury began to swirl in her stomach, and no matter how hard she sucked in air the motion picked up pace like a cyclone. 'Now, just wait a minute—'

'You have no regard for your safety. None,' he said with a slash of his hands. 'I have seen safer streets in the slums.

Well, I will tell you this right now. We are not staying here. *Comprende?*'

Her mouth shaping for a scathing retort along the lines of *It's none of your damn business,* she felt his words loop round her skull like a broken record. Her hand crept up to her throat, where her pulse jumped erratically. 'What do you mean, *we?*'

'From the time you agreed to the terms to the time we arrive at the Arunthian palace you are under *my* protection,' he grated, seemingly not entirely happy with the prospect.

Well, neither was she!

'Next time you barter with me, Claudia, you'd better think twice about the consequences. For the next twenty-four hours we are stuck together. Whether you like it or not.'

Oh, God. As Shakespeare might say, she'd been hoist with her own petard.

'Clearly you don't,' she said. She felt sick. She felt dizzy. Was it physically possible to strangle yourself?

'I have better things to do than babysit a self-centred, sense-less, se… *Arrrrggh.*' With a frustrated roar, he pushed open the car door and launched himself from the bucket seat. Before he'd even slammed it shut she yanked on the handle to follow him. And finally the rotten thing worked!

'Whoa—wait a minute,' she said, veering round the front bonnet, sloshing in puddles. Freezing water seeped into her shoes, while the rain lashed down to drench her hair and pummel her skin. Vision blurring, she pushed her glasses on top of her head, visor-like. 'Where I live has *nothing* to do with you.' By the time she'd caught up to him he was pacing back and forth on the walkway in his usual caged predator manner. 'You barge into my life and proceed to conduct some sort of military operation. And now you're going on like an interfering, dictatorial knave!'

Suddenly he stopped and turned on his heels to face her. 'Do you have an aversion to authority, Claudia? Is that what this is? You don't like being told what to do?'

The grey silken weave of his sartorial suit darkened to almost black as huge rain droplets seeped through his clothing. His over-long hair was already dripping, plastered to his smooth forehead and the high slash of his cheekbones. And— *oh, my*—the sight of him, wet and dishevelled, flooded her core with heat. Like this he was far more powerful and dangerous to her equilibrium. He looked roguish, gloriously untamed.

Her heart thumping so hard she could hear her pulse echo in her ears, she had to scroll back to remember what he'd said. *Oh, yeah. The brute.*

'No, actually, I don't. Do you think it's right to force someone against their every wish? To blackmail in order to do your job?' Something dark flashed in his eyes but she was too far gone to care. 'And because I dare to put up some sort of fight you deem me selfish and irresponsible. Do you have *any* feelings?'

'I am not paid to feel,' he ground out, taking a step closer towards her.

'It's a good job, 'cos you'd be broke,' she replied, taking a step back.

Lucas pinched the bridge of his nose with his thumb and forefinger. 'You are the most provoking woman I have ever met.'

A mere two feet away, Claudia could feel the heat radiating from his broad torso. Oh, God, she had to get away from him before she did something seriously stupid. Like smooth her hands up his soaked shirt. 'You know what, Lucas? You can sleep in your posh car for all I care. Frankly, I've been more comfortable on the 271 bus from Highgate. I'm staying here.'

Before he could say another word she bolted sideways. Only to be blocked by a one-arm barricade.

'Over my dead body,' he growled, corralling her back towards the car.

'That could be arranged,' she said, suddenly breathless.

Rain poured down her face, her throat, to trickle down the inside of her collar. That was why she shuddered so hard. It had nothing to do with the fact that Lucas was inching towards her with lethal intent.

'You are coming with me. From now on I am in charge.'

'Well, you can just rid yourself of *that* illusion. You'll never be in charge of me!'

Suddenly her back connected with the car in a wet slap and she felt the engine thunder and roar with its need to unleash power. The vibration shot up her spine and then pinballed back down her vertebrae, surging for every extremity until she felt like a pulsing livewire.

'You know what, Claudia?'

It was his hot, heavy tone more than his words that caught her attention, and she jerked up to catch the feral gleam in his eyes.

'Wha…what?'

Water streamed down his brow, dripped off his nose and lingered on his darkening jaw as she hung on his every word. After swiping his face with deft hands he shook his head, like a dog shedding its bath, to send even more rain showering over her.

Hot and sultry liquid pooled in her abdomen and she pushed against the cool metal to stop herself from sliding into a heap at his feet. The awesome sight of him was distressing enough, but for some reason Claudia wished he were utterly naked. Well, not totally. Maybe just his top half. So she could take a peek. *Oh, God,* what was happening to her?

'I am beginning to think I've handled you all wrong,' he said, licking his lips hungrily. 'I have been a negotiator,' he said, holding up one finger. 'Waste of time and effort.'

Her eyes were glued to his sensual mouth, mesmerised by the way his wet lips moved as he spoke. He had great teeth.

'I have tried to appeal to your better nature,' he continued, holding two fingers up. 'However, I'm not at all sure you have one.'

'Hey, that's not fair—'

He silenced her with two warm fingers and her cool flesh

sizzled on contact. It took every ounce of self-control to stop herself licking. Nibbling.

'I have even tried kid gloves and allowing you to barter for extra time. And look where that has brought us. To a hovel in one of the scummiest areas I have ever had the displeasure to visit.'

Lucas dragged his fingers over her mouth, the pressure curling her bottom lip and tugging her eyelids shut. 'This is a nice area. You're just a snob,' she breathed.

'I should have hauled you out of that lab hours ago,' he said, his volume lower, his tone silkier. 'Straight onto a plane and straight home to Arunthia. This is what I get for being considerate.'

Oh, he *had* to be joking!

Her eyes flew open. He was staring at her mouth, following her tongue as it licked her lips over and over in basic instinct. The fresh taste of Mother Nature blended with bittersweet anticipation. 'You're an animal. A...a beast.'

'You know what else, *Just Claudia?* I think there's only one way to shut you up.'

Bracing his hands against the car on either side of her, he leaned forward, eyes glittering.

Oooh, my. Her heart kicked into overdrive. Her blood fizzed through her veins. A strange bearing down in her abdomen forced her to clench her insides, the slight twitch making her core spasm with liquid fever.

Lucas's body heat burned through her wet clothing and she trembled so violently that her words—'You wouldn't dare...'—came out more like a plea.

Hitching a dark, sexy brow, he murmured. 'Ah, Claudia, didn't anyone ever tell you never to provoke an animal?'

CHAPTER FOUR

ANIMAL.

The word assaulted his brain, fighting to break through the heady maelstrom of anger and high-octane sexual desire. Blinking rapidly, every shuttering of his eyes brought another aspect of their surroundings into sharper relief.

London. Unsafe. Protect.

They were soaked to the skin. Claudia's grey Mac moulded to the swell of her full, high breasts with every shivery breath she took. Minuscule drops of rain beaded on her long lashes like black diamonds, and as her eyes fluttered the rare gems lost their precarious hold and trickled down her beautiful face.

She slowly opened her eyes and focused on his mouth. She rose on her toes and her breasts grazed up his chest. His groin hardened to titanium as the moisture sizzled on his skin.

Dios, what was she doing? More to the point, what was *he* doing? She made him lose his mind, his self-control, and at this rate he would be *sans* all honour by Monday next.

Retreat, Garcia. Retreat. Now!

She stilled, flicked her big amber eyes up to his, and what he saw nearly shocked his heart into cardiac arrest. Fear. She was scared. Of *him.*

Animal.

'No.' *Never.*

This was his idea of protection? Crowding her against the side of a car in the sheeting rain?

'Apologies, Your Royal Highness,' he said, pushing off the car and taking three large paces back.

'Don't call me that,' she whispered.

A deep V creased her brow as she searched his face, then took a keen interest in her feet. If it were anyone else he would think she was disappointed but, *Dios,* the fear.

He had to remember who she was, even if she didn't quite grasp the fact. Why the hell was she living in this cesspool? For the sake of a twenty-minute taxi-ride to work? No, he doubted it. But now was not the time to cause further animosity. He needed her to listen and obey him. If she could just do as she was told for five minutes things would get a hell of a lot easier.

'Claudia, get in the car. I need to get you dry. Away from this place.'

'I don't mind being wet. I love the rain. So pure and clean.' Chin lifting, she tipped her face skyward. 'I can't remember the last time I did this.'

His eyes traced the graceful line of her throat and his heart thumped back to life. The abysmal weather had failed to diminish the colour of her lustrous gold-toned skin—her Arunthian heritage.

'I am very glad,' he murmured, his fingers howling to stroke her silken cheek. Claudia's face plummeted back to his and he realised he must have spoken out loud. *Damn.* 'I do not think delivering you home with a bout of pneumonia would go in my favour.'

Her lips curved ruefully. 'Of course.' She stood tall, swiped her forehead with the back of her hand to brush tendrils of hair from her temple, and glanced up to the building behind him. 'I can go and change, but I haven't got anything for you, I'm afraid.'

The tense muscle in his shoulders eased as she inadvertently gave away her lack of live-in-lover status. Of course that didn't mean she was single. And collating all the facts was his job, was it not?

'My clothing is of no consequence.' Compared to being

caked in three months' worth of dirt sweat and blood, a little water was exiguous. 'Please—lead the way.'

She swung her gaze back to him, eyes wide. 'I can manage perfectly well myself. Just give me five minutes—'

'No. I will accompany you. You'll need more than five minutes to pack. Then we'll spend the night in the Thames apartment.'

Her eyes grew impossibly larger. 'We can't do that.'

'Why not?'

'Well…because it's empty.'

He groaned, long and low, clenching his fists to stop himself from giving her a damn good shake. 'And your post? Letters? They are forwarded…yes?'

She nibbled on her plump bottom lip. 'No. Come to think of it, I haven't picked them up for months. I've been so busy.'

Dios, little wonder her father's letters had gained no reply. But why warmth rushed through him at the realisation he had no idea.

'No matter. I will extend my stay at the Astoria. We'll stay there for the night.'

'I don't want to stay there.' Tugging at her cuffs, she tossed her head in an aggravating lofty flounce. 'I can just stay here.'

Head snapping upright, he gave her *The Look.* The look designed to command hundreds of soldiers and stop assassins in their tracks.

And what did she do? Rolled her amber eyes!

'Fine,' she said. 'But for heaven's sake don't use that look on me again. It will never work.' She caught a yawn in her small fist. 'I'm just so tired I can barely think straight, let alone argue with you.'

She looked past tired, but he had no intention of taking the blame for her ferocious work ethic or any other night-time activities she indulged in.

'This is progress indeed. Keys?' he said, palm outstretched.

She dug into her pocket, rummaging. Out came a tissue, a

pencil, a small notepad. All of which she stuffed in her free hand. 'I know I picked them up. I *know* I did.'

Raking his hair back from his face, he took a moment to rein in his anxiety. And in that instant an arrow of ice speared up his nape and his head snapped upright.

Traffic weaved around his parked car—a black hatchback, a red coupe—and beyond, on the opposite side of the street, there was a small Italian restaurant, a run-down clothes store, a church. And, parked directly in front, a large white pick-up.

'Get in the car.'

'What?' she said, delving into her other pocket.

'Now!'

'Do you have to be so impatient? I'm telling you the rotten key is in here somewhere.'

Lucas gripped her arm, ignored the pocket paraphernalia clattering to the pavement, marched her round the car, opened the door and pushed her inside.

'Lucas, really,' she said, poking her head out. 'What is *wrong* with you?'

Palm flat on top of her head, he pressed her back into the car, slammed the door, ate the tarmac in five quick paces and folded his frame into the seat beside her. 'Buckle up.'

'No. I need to go inside,' she said, exasperated, pointing at the red brick façade of her grotty flat. 'I don't have any—'

'Claudia, I do not care what you want. We are being watched, and I need to get you out of here.'

'Watched?' she repeated, in a high-pitched squeak as her hand crept up her chest and wrapped around the base of her throat. 'But that's impossible. No one knows me.'

Yesterday that might have been true, but when the Arunthian King disclosed his intent to gather the royal family for the event of the decade things changed. Lucas had known that. Which was why he'd flown into a military base. Why he hadn't ordered chauffeur-driven cars. When the King's three daughters were dotted around the globe, and in particular when one had been missing for well over a decade, interest was ripe.

Claudia was spoken of in hushed tones, and in all his years working for the King he'd never been told her exact whereabouts. Until now. He didn't envy her the scrutiny she'd be placed under when they returned. Only the best guards would be selected to watch over her, and Lucas would ensure he chose men with eyes in the back of their heads—for she was nothing but reckless obstinacy.

His mind flitting through the options, he took one last glance at the white pick-up truck.

'Unless…' she said.

Lucas pulled out into the lane of traffic, feeling her eyes burning into the side of his face. He knew what was coming—could feel the initial flare of her wrath. Perversely, it began to stoke the fires he'd managed to douse.

'Oh, my God,' she said, elbows bent, fingers pressing into her temples like one of those telepaths harnessing their brain power. 'You know what, Lucas? I've known of your existence for three hours and already my life has gone to the dogs. There's only one reason for someone to take a sudden interest in me. *You've* blown my cover!'

Lucas slapped the indicator and gripped the steering wheel until his knuckles ached. *Dios,* how had this happened? For the first time in his career he'd failed to do his job. First by almost kissing her and second by putting her in jeopardy. Within five seconds of their meeting he'd lost control of his carnal appetites and his instincts were sloth-like. How long had the pick-up truck been standing there? While he, the Head of Security, had had her hard up against a car, ready to devour her mouth and anything else he could reach.

'I cannot see how,' he said, vexed as he attempted to find an explanation for this strange phenomenon. 'Do you think me so inept I would announce my arrival in the country to the press?'

'How do I know if you're any good at your job? So far I've been blackmailed, shouted at and suffered a good soaking.'

Good point.

From the corner of his eye he watched her yank her glasses

from atop her head and rub the lenses on her coat. Her sodden coat.

'Great. Now I don't even have a tissue because you—' She took a deep breath and tossed the thick frames into the footwell. 'Anyway, how do you know…?' He heard her audible gulp. 'That they were press.'

'I only suspect,' he said, knowing his hunch was enough. It always had been. Apart from that one time. When he'd lost everything. When he'd been ruled by emotion—something that would never, *ever* happen again. Emotion made you sloppy. Careless.

Lucas ignored the crucifying scratch of his conscience, warning him of the similarities to his current predicament. This was different. *This* was a dire case of sexual chemistry messing with his head.

'Well, forgive me if I don't share in your suspicions. You could be overreacting. There are hundreds of vans in London. Thousands, in fact. No one has ever given me a second glance.'

'*Dios,* Claudia, that's because no one knows who you are. You are hidden well in London and you purposely dress in camouflage.'

'I don't purposely dress in anything. I dress for comfort and my personal taste.'

He snorted, and was about to tell her that against all evidence to the contrary he was not a stupid man when he glanced in his rearview mirror.

'Push your spine into the seat and look straight ahead. I need to lose my *suspicious overreaction* and take some swift turns.'

'Oh, good grief. Could this day get any worse?' she said, her fingers curling around the leather lip of the seat alongside her slender thighs.

Sí. He could have kissed her.

And if that thought wasn't bad enough, they lost the van within three minutes only to get snarled up in traffic—while Claudia caught yawn after yawn in her small fist.

'You need sleep,' he said, frowning at the dark smudges beneath her eyes. 'You look ill.'

'Why, thank you, Lucas,' she said, voice dripping with sarcasm. 'Just what I wanted to hear.'

In his peripheral vision he watched her rub the outer flesh of her thighs for the third time and his foul mood ratcheted up a notch. Why did his brain insist on informing him of every damn move she made?

'Next you'll tell me we're still being *followed*.'

Why didn't she believe him? Never had his word been questioned. The knock to his honour gave his tone extra bite. 'No. You may rest.'

Lucas determinedly switched off, focused on changing gear and lowering his pulse. Soon enough he pulled into the private rear entrance of the Astoria and watched daylight being eclipsed by the metal security doors until only a thin sliver remained. Extinguishing the engine, he glanced over at Claudia. Her head was cushioned by the soft leather padded wing, her eyes were closed, breathing steady and even. In peace, her beauty was breathtaking.

Eyes trailing down her body, his guts twisted at the sight of damp cloth sticking to her skin, outlining her lush curves.

'Claudia?' he said—loud enough to wake the dead. Otherwise he'd have no choice but to touch her, and while his body was willing and able his mind rejected the idea immediately.

The problem was, where Claudia was concerned his body seemed to rule. Why else would he be in this imbroglio in the first place? He should have her ensconced in the jet by now, halfway to Arunthia. Perfectly dry and unruffled.

Unfortunately it seemed his reluctant royal was dead to the world.

'*Dios.*' Lucas thrust open his door and launched himself to his feet, adrenaline pumping through his body and making him hard all over.

Barking orders to the security guard to clear his path, he

scooped her into his arms and strode through the darkened corridors, ordering his body not to feel. Not to react.

Damn impossible when she curled into his arms, snuggled against his damp chest, laid her head on his broad shoulder and grabbed fistfuls of his white shirt. Heat shot down his spine, pooled in his groin, and by the time he reached the penthouse his heart was thumping a twenty-man stampede that had nothing to do with exertion.

The guard opened the door to the penthouse and Lucas marched to the enormous bed, laid her down and backed the *hell* away.

'Sir? Do you need any further assistance?'

Lucas scrubbed his jaw. 'Clothes. She needs something dry to sleep in.' Why hadn't he thought of this? What did women sleep in apart from their skin? Gorgeous honey-gold skin… His throat turned thick as molasses along with his blood, and against a direct order his eyes toppled back to the bed.

'We have a concession downstairs, sir. I could ask one of the assistants to help?'

He nodded, heard the man exit the room with a decisive click and reached for his mobile phone. He was determined to find the man who'd followed them, and soon, but first… *Dios,* she was in serious danger of becoming ill.

Claudia was curling her long body into a foetal position on the gold coverlet, and he was smacked with that hint of vulnerability once more. His mind latched onto another woman at another time. Defenceless. Frail. Unprotected. By him.

Lucas clenched his stomach to stop the pain ripping his abdomen clean in half, reached for the plateau he visited in the dead of night and banished the memory.

Gritting his teeth, he focused on Claudia, curled his hand round her soft upper arm and gently tugged her onto her back. The sight of her stretching sinuously against the satin was one adrenaline shot to his groin too many. Cursing, he began to pop her coat buttons from top to bottom, peeling away the layers, trying his utmost to stay disconnected, yet unable to deny the tremor of his fingers.

Then, *gracias a Dios,* she murmured and began to stir, turning on her side.

'Claudia? Wake up. I need you to take off your clothes.'

'Okay,' she murmured sleepily, as she rolled back on her side and buried her face in the palm of her hand.

'No. No! Do not sleep. Not yet.'

That did it. She opened her eyes. Blinked. Stretched again. Writhed her centrefold body like the she-devil she was. Then bolted upright. 'Where am I?'

'In my hotel suite. You may sleep, but first you need to undress,' he said, his already tentative hold on control fraying at the image of her undressing in front of him. *For* him.

Her face scrunching in a strangely pretty grimace, she twisted her legs, folding them underneath her. 'Ugh, I feel horrid,' she said, absorbing her surroundings, her eyes wide as they flew to his. 'How did I get up here?'

'I carried you. In slumber you bring new meaning to the adage sleeping like the dead.'

Cheeks pinkening, she swung her legs over the edge of the bed, her eyes riveted to his chest. 'Oh, I know. Comes from sleeping in the noisiest places.' At his quizzical glance she elaborated. 'In a hospital full of children with paper-thin walls. Still, I'm surprised you managed it.'

'Are you?' Was it his imagination or did she fixate on his chest a little too long?

'No, not really. You're huge.'

Her voice was husky but he managed to put that down to thirst. The alternative was a treacherous road to travel down.

'I'd bet good money you're the only man on the planet who could manage it, though.'

Plenty of his men could—not that he'd ever allow it. The thought unearthed a foreign sensation in his guts. 'You are far from heavy, Claudia. I have carried twice your weight on my back for days on end.'

'Why on earth would you do that?'

Thuds began to pound at his temples. 'Up,' he ordered, amazed that he'd told her that. Frankly astounded that he'd divulged one iota of his past. *Dios,* he needed to get rid of her. 'I've decided that we should return to Arunthia today.'

But she wasn't listening. Something had occurred in her fierce brain. 'Oh, of course. How silly of me. I saw it straight away too. You're military. Or ex-military at least.'

She attempted to stand but fell straight back onto her rear. A curvaceous bottom now imprinted on his forearm—lush and firm.

A groan rumbled up his chest but he managed to stall it halfway up his windpipe.

'And, by the way, you can forget leaving today. You promised me twenty-four hours, Mr Garcia.'

She stood then, unfolding to her full height: a phoenix rising from the flames.

'I was under the impression I was dealing with a man of his word.' *Ouch.*

'I'm not leaving until tomorrow. I have business to attend to in London, tomorrow morning, and I'll be there. Fire, flood or obnoxious control-freak notwithstanding.'

Lucas fumed from the inside out. 'There is every chance we will be followed again.' He'd make sure they were not, but he had no intention of making her feel comfortable. She should be concerned for her safety, dammit. She was in for a rude awakening back at home.

'*If* we were followed. I'll chance it.'

'Still you continue to doubt my word.' What could possibly be so important for her to even risk it?

She met his eyes, tore on her lip. And he knew. It must be a man. The thought struck a knife to his heart. Dragged him back into the darkness. Why did women do this to themselves? Jeopardise their life for a man?

'You may be willing to chance it but I am not,' he said, hard enough to ram the point into the next millennium. 'You have ten seconds to tell me what or who is so important. Then I promise you, Claudia, the decision will be mine.'

Her stunned mouth worked. 'But…you gave me your word.'

Lucas moved in, slowly biting out each syllable. 'I will break it in a heartbeat if your safety is in question.'

She slumped back onto the bed and stared up at him. 'You mean it.'

'I am *deadly* serious.' He'd had enough. Of her blasé attitude. Of the constant spike of his pulse. Of the fact that he'd forgone his word of honour for her protection as a result of her sheer obstinacy. Of everything *Claudia*. 'You have less than five seconds.'

Her eyes widened.

'Four.'

'I have to see someone,' she said, her words rushing out as she covered her heart with the palm of her hand.

'Not enough. Three.'

'I promised, okay? I can't just disappear. You've smashed into my life with the delicacy of a ten-ton brick. I have to see her before I leave.'

'Two. Her?' he asked, slightly mollified by the sex of this person.

'Bailey…she would be devastated. This is a huge deal to me, Lucas. *Please*.'

Clenching his fists, he eased back. Maybe if she hadn't been looking up to him, with those heart-achingly beautiful eyes pleading. Maybe if he hadn't seen the effort it had taken her.

Tamping down on the emotion flickering inside him, he motioned towards the bathroom door with a jerk of his head. 'If you can manage a hot shower, there is a robe on the back of the door. Then we will eat and you may sleep.'

Her entire body wilted. 'I *may?*' she said, a smile quivering about her lips.

Lucas imagined it was half pleasure that he'd granted her

leeway and half indignation that he was calling the shots. She had spunk. He'd give her that.

'*Sí*. You *may*.'

Claudia closed the bathroom door, turned and slumped against the solid oak.

'That man is killing me softly,' she whispered. He was so stern his icy orders could freeze a running tap mid-flow, yet he'd agreed to let her visit Bailey *and* carried her from the car. Although she imagined in that instance he'd acted on automatic, and the experience had been as pleasurable for him as being tear-gassed.

Groaning, Claudia pushed away from the door and began to unpeel her sticky clothes from her skin. After kicking off her shoes, she wriggled out of her tights and panties, glancing around the huge plush bathroom.

A black clawfoot tub sat on cream tiles luxuriously warm under her now bare feet. Walking over to the shower, she unbuttoned her lab coat with one hand and turned the shower dial with the other, until steam began to pour over the glass wall—shaped in a slinky S—and filled the room, blissfully warming every inch of skin she unveiled.

Shallow twin basins took up one wall and, unsnapping her bra, she walked over to peek inside the huge complimentary basket, wrinkling her nose at the visual feast. God only knew what products were in there. Before she got a decent look she was snagged on her condensation-hazy reflection in the wide mirror above the ceramic bowls.

'Oh, lovely!' Colour high, clumps of dark-brown hair hanging about her face, huge puffy bags under her eyes: she looked like a human panda bear. Was it any wonder Lucas looked at her as if she were half-mad? She certainly acted half-mad around him.

Grimacing, she closed her eyes, and her mind drifted to a close-up of Lucas, towering above her, as she was plastered to his car. Who was the woman who'd reached up for his kiss? So sure she'd been. So *wrong* she'd been. He'd been furious, attempting to show her who was boss. A man like Lucas wouldn't be interested in her. His women would be lithe, glamorous, *über*-confident. Everything Claudia wasn't.

Sadness crept into her chest until each breath ached and she gently rubbed her wrist, her eyes wavering on the basket. He might not fancy her, but she didn't have to look a fright in front of him, did she? Snagging a bottle of shampoo, she dipped into the shower. The hot splash of water firmed her resolve. She had twenty-four hours to get her head on straight, visit Bailey and fly home to face her parents for the first time in years.

Suddenly it didn't matter what Lucas thought of her. What mattered was that her mask didn't slip in front of him. In front of any of them. Staying strong, she had more chance of getting back to London, with her body, mind and soul untouched.

So when she strode out of the bathroom twenty minutes later, a towel wrapped turban-like around her head and cloaked in a huge white robe, she was armed and ready. Sort of. As long as she ignored the scent of Lucas seeping through the thick cotton, infusing her extreme nakedness with what she imagined a lover's caress would feel like.

Bedroom empty, she took a deep breath and strode through the open doorway into a lavish Victorian-style living area— and stopped dead.

Lucas stood with his back to her, looking out of the wide expanse of windows offering a spectacular view of the fading Thames skyline. A dark blue shirt clung to his broad shoulders, stretching tight as he bent at the waist and reached down. Claudia couldn't care less what was on the floor. Her eyes were riveted to the small of his back leading to a very tight butt. *Wow.* Her vision began to swim; maybe she had brain fever.

She heard him firing orders like soft bullets. Strangely subdued, she couldn't make out the words, but the low growl of his voice made her insides quake. The base of her stomach fluttered and a honeyed whimper floated past her ears.

Brow furrowing, she wrenched her gaze towards the door,

only to be faced with…a *woman?* A woman failing miserably at hiding her own response: cheeks overly pink, finger stroking her small cleavage as she checked out Lucas for herself.

Claudia stifled the impulse to tell the impeccably dressed blonde to get out. 'Can I help you?'

Three things happened. Lucas whipped around. The blonde dropped a coat hanger to the floor. And Claudia fisted the lapels of her gown together at the base of her throat, suddenly wishing she'd kept her mouth shut and left the way she'd come. Given her current panda bear appearance, being faced with a sultry cat was more than she could take.

'Ah, Claudia. *Finally,*' Lucas said. 'This is Jessica from the concession downstairs. She has clothes for you.'

Not a chance. 'Can't we just send my clothes to be cleaned?'

A muscle ticked along his jaw and he set stride towards her. She stiffened, bracing herself.

'Give us five minutes,' he said to the blonde, who nodded and then disappeared into another room.

'Doesn't she know where the door is?'

'This is not the time for your awkwardness,' he growled for her ears only, so close she shuddered.

Determined not to look at him, she kept her eyes fixed on the clothes rail. 'How is it awkward not to want new clothes?' God, how ungrateful she sounded. She couldn't remember the last time anyone had thought of her needs—was too used to fighting for them herself. 'I do appreciate the gesture, Lucas, but…' The rail sagged beneath the weight of tens of hangers adorned with a colourful array of every garment imaginable. She swallowed. Hard.

'You wish to wear a lab coat on your journey home?' he asked, exasperation hardening his voice.

'Maybe I could pop back to my flat later? I just want my own things.'

'*Dios,* Claudia, give it up,' he snapped. 'I doubt there is anything suitable in that place. There is no need to hide here. I know who you are.'

Her head jerked so quickly a spasm catapulted up her neck. Standing no more than a foot away he looked furious. 'What are you talking about?'

'I understand the need for dour camouflage while you are in London. But from this moment on everyone you meet will know exactly who you are. I will make sure of it.'

She blinked. Took a step back. Then another. Why did her heart shrivel in her chest because he thought her appearance dour?

His brow etched into a deep V, the skin around his eyes crinkling, he scoured her face. Claudia looked back to the rail and crushed the hurt before he could witness it.

'Fine,' she said, proud of her unwavering voice. 'One outfit.' Truth be told she had little choice in the matter. It was clear she wouldn't be permitted to return home, and surely there was *something* among this glut that wasn't…skimpy.

Lucas cleared his throat. 'Do you wish to sleep in that robe?' he asked, a little softer, silkier, while his eyes slid down her body in a bold visual caress, as if he craved to see her extreme nakedness beneath. *As if.*

'Sleep in it?' Hardly. Not with *his* woodsy scent lingering on every fibre. 'I think not. And do me a favour and stop staring at me. I realise I'm not your standard issue—'

A knock at the door severed her tongue. Both their heads turned in the same direction.

'Why do I suddenly feel like I'm standing in the middle of King's Cross Station?' Butt naked!

She adhered her feet to the floor in case she edged closer to Lucas. She'd never needed anyone and she didn't need him now.

A pause. Two raps. And a beat. A pattern, she realised. 'Forget King's Cross. I'm in the Arunthian Intelligence Agency.'

'Enter,' Lucas barked, his lips twitching, and Claudia stepped back a pace when another incredible hunk strode through the gap.

'Good grief. Your brother?'

Lucas coughed into his fist. 'One of my men. Armande. And I do not believe we are alike.'

The man—Armande—bowed in front of her. 'Your Royal Highness.' He straightened to resemble a ramrod and nodded at Lucas. 'Sir.'

'No, you're right. He seems too nice,' she whispered, so only Lucas could hear.

Lucas had ordered clothes. Been thoughtful. Agreed to let her see Bailey. Carried her from the car. Cared for her. He needn't have done that, she realised. He could have woken her up. Ordered her to walk.

She shivered from the top of her turbanned head to the tips of her toes just thinking about his big strong arms embracing her, holding her tight, snug against his chest. Wasn't it just typical that she'd slept the entire time? She wanted a replay.

Unmindful, her eyes sought his. He was staring at her mouth again, at where she gnawed at the flesh of her lip with her front teeth. Then he looked to Armande…back to her…and his jaw set rigid.

'Armande is in charge for now,' he said, strangely ill-tempered. 'I have something to take care of.'

'*What?*' Turning her back on Armande, she instinctively latched onto Lucas's forearm. 'You're leaving me? With…with *him?*'

He frowned, flicked his attention to her white-knuckled grip. 'You'll be perfectly safe.'

'Are you coming back?' She did *not* sound needy—definitely not. She sounded inquisitive.

'*Sí.* Of course.'

How many times had she heard that? Too many. Yet for some reason she believed him. Who in their right mind would coerce her into going to Arunthia only to abandon her before the flight?

She slackened her hold, feeling like a total idiot. 'Fine. I'm going to bed anyway.'

'One hour,' he declared, before dipping his head discreetly towards her ear.

Stomach fizzing, she clenched her lower abdomen and sucked her tender bottom lip. His breath tickled down the sensitive skin of her neck, his husky murmur igniting each tiny fizzy bubble until it exploded inside her.

'Try to behave yourself, *Just Claudia*.'

CHAPTER FIVE

'ALONE?' LUCAS SAID, satisfied with his controlled volume as he lowered the morning newspaper to the breakfast table and sent Claudia *The Look*.

Dark insolent brows arched in his direction before she sipped pure orange juice between her ripe lips. A direct order from God couldn't have stopped him from watching her slender throat convulse, her pink tongue snake out to lick the pith sticking to her perfect bow. The newspaper crumpled in his fist as heat snaked through his veins, making his pulse spike.

'Yes, Lucas. I want to go alone.'

He cleared his throat. 'Impossible. I will accompany you or you will not go. End of discussion.'

Keeping his paper lowered, he waited for her reaction, but the ice maiden had risen with the morning sun.

Dressed in a sharp, fitted black suit, her hair tied back punishingly into a twisted knot, she looked a world away from the dowdy lab rat of yesterday. Still, every inch of her skin was covered, the only break in the black a fawn shirt, stroking her decolletage. Satin, he mused, eyeing the way the expensive fabric rippled around her neck. Today she had an untouchable, regal aura—one he was extremely grateful for.

'Why are you staring at me? Do I look *dour* this morning?'

Lucas jerked his eyes back to her face. Had he just imagined her wounded tone? With his limited experience of the female sex outside the sheets he felt unsure how to proceed. *Unsure? Dios,* he felt something close to panic claw down his chest. Never had he been asked to comment on a woman's appearance.

Lucas snapped the paper shut and laid it on the table beside his empty coffee cup. 'Not at all. I was just thinking how smart you look.'

'Smart?' she repeated, deadpan, tapping her pencil off her front teeth, popping the end into her mouth and nibbling it.

He shifted in his seat. '*Sí.* Appropriate for your arrival in Arunthia.'

'I'm not there yet,' she said, no more happy with his comment than he was.

Damn. He should have told her she was beautiful. How he itched to untie her hair, to caress her long, sultry curls.

As it was, the memory of a hard floor against his back and a walking centrefold in the cushy bed thirty feet away would haunt him for days. By four a.m. he'd done six hundred situps, cleaned his gun, had three showers and interviewed the man in the white pick-up. Armande had hauled the bastard into the adjoining suite at midnight. A shifty Arunthian reporter whom Lucas had despised on sight. One who wouldn't be returning to his home country for some time. Not as long as Claudia was there.

The reminder brought him back to her comment. She wasn't in Arunthia. *Yet.*

'Our flight is at three p.m. You have plenty of time to make your visit. Accompanied,' he tagged on, unwilling to be moved on the point.

Tearing at a slice of wholemeal toast, she chewed with vigour and speared him with arrows of contempt.

Good. She hated him. As long as he kept that look on her face they'd make it home without another hitch. Problem was Lucas had an uneasy notion that Claudia was about to produce a hitch the size of Mount Vesuvius.

* * *

'There is something wrong with you?' asked Lucas, with a harshness that made Claudia's skin bristle.

Sliding her eyes over the vast entrance of St Andrew's Hospital, she knotted her fingers atop her lap.

What? Was he concerned that he'd have to take damaged goods through Security in Arunthia? Claudia would laugh if the chord didn't strike through to the very heart of her. How many times had she dreamed of being perfect, being cured, just so her parents would come back for her? Days, months, years spent waiting, her naïve heart still hoping.

Throat thick, pain smashing into her forehead, she rubbed her brow with an unsteady hand. Why couldn't she forget? Why couldn't she just get over it and move on?

'Claudia? Answer me!'

She turned to look at a scowling Lucas in the seat beside her, hating the instant fire in her belly just one look ignited. 'No, Lucas, there is nothing wrong with me. Apart from the insane urge to strangle you.' The man was driving her to Valium.

Scowl diminishing, a smile played about his lips. 'The feeling is entirely mutual, *princesa*. So, tell me, why are we here?'

'I sometimes work here and—'

He snorted, relief easing the two little lines he got when he frowned. 'I should have known.'

'Actually, on this occasion it isn't about work. I was about to say I met someone here. Bailey, remember? So if you'll excuse me—'

'Wait,' he said, grasping her wrist.

Whether it was the hundred volts ripping up her arm or the fact he'd touched her wrist, she wasn't sure, but she twisted her arm, writhing from his hold. 'Please don't touch me there.'

Lucas instantly let go and held up his hand. 'I would not hurt you, Claudia,' he said, voice gruff, his brows low over intense eyes brimming with...*pain?* Oh, no. *No!*

'Of course you wouldn't.' No thought, no hesitation, she

reached over, lightly grazing his fist where it now curled on his hard thigh. His skin was so warm. So perfect. 'I know that.'

'*Bueno*. Good,' he said, his chest visibly easing.

Yes, he was hard—but in a warrior-like way. Good fighting against evil.

And that one thought…the mere possibility that he might have faced evil…coupled with that one agonised look derailed her pride, her every defence. 'I'm just really funny about my wrists. That's all. And when…' *When you touch me I feel alive. For the first time in my life. And it scares me.*

Those beautiful sapphire eyes flicked down to where her fingers still smoothed over his flesh and his hand slowly began to stiffen as if repelled.

Hurt kissed her heart and she snatched her hand back. 'Anyway, I need to go inside.'

Lucas reached for the door handle. '*Sí*. We will go,' he said, fierce, dominating, as if the moment had never happened.

The change in him was so swift it took her a moment to gather her wits. '*We?* No, Lucas. That's not acceptable.'

She wouldn't put Bailey through a meeting with a stranger. She remembered all too well the pity. The staring. The crushing silence that seemed to stretch the air so thin she could barely breathe. The powerful desire for them to leave followed by the stomach-wrenching emptiness of the room. And just as unforgettable was the palpable unease of others. It wasn't fair on Lucas either.

'Claudia, you are in my protection,' he ground out.

'For once will you stop thinking about your bloody job and give me an hour's peace before my life is obliterated? I need to see someone. In private. Can't you understand that?'

Lucas tore his gaze from the grim scenery and narrowed his eyes on her. 'You feel deeply for this person?'

'Yes. Just an hour. Please?'

The shutters slammed down over his face. 'One hour. I will wait.'

'Thank you.'

'In Reception.'

'*Reception?* People are sure to ask questions as soon as they clap eyes on you. You're hardly inconspicuous.'

He shrugged those broad muscular shoulders. 'Tough.'

'God, you're the most arrogant louse I've ever met.' And to think she'd just told him something she'd never told another soul just to make him feel better.

Pushing her glasses up her nose, she yanked her bag from the floor as the car door opened before her. And there stood Lucas.

'How…? You know something? You're the human equivalent of a silencer.'

He flashed her a killer half-smile. 'One hour, *Just Claudia.*'

Lucas paced the reception area, his size twelves wearing holes in the thin matting, and yanked back the cuff of his jacket to check his watch. Again. One hour, seven minutes, thirty-six seconds.

Dios, he abhorred hospitals: the thick air of grief sliding down his throat, the dread, the notion that control had been handed to God and Lucas would pay the price.

Teeth bared, he let out a low growl. Where the hell *was* she? And who was this Bailey person? A lover? She'd intimated a female, but he knew women lied under the dense weight of desperation.

Anger swirled, black and heavy in his gut, as well as some indefinable emotion he was loath to name. The suspicion sparked a flare of unease in him. Was she safe? The shock of it suddenly engulfed him and acted like an almighty trigger.

He strode towards the curved reception desk, set like a barricade, denying all further access to the floors beyond. Her private business was no concern of his but, *Dios,* one hour was one hour, and if something happened to her…

After flashing a smile to the emaciated blonde, some extreme lash-fluttering, flaunting his government credentials and name-dropping his right-royal-pain-in-the-ass, she directed him to floor seven and one Bailey Michaels.

Adrenaline surged to every extremity until he felt hard—armed and ready to take on the world as he stalked towards the lift, then bypassed it for the stairs, needing to run off some excess energy, throwing open the doors to the seventh floor a minute later.

Three things happened simultaneously to punch the air from his lungs. The musical sound of children's voices floated past his ears. The colourful images of cartoon characters painted on vast glass plates drew his eyes. And the scent of strong disinfectant speared up his nose to assault his mind.

Stomach revolting, he stiffened his abs to prevent his six-egg omelette from making a reappearance. Twenty years vanished and he was back in the halls of hell.

His hand shot out to grip the wooden ledge framing a window. His thoughts fractured. His vision blurred. Air was imprisoned in his chest. *Get up, boy. I'm not done. Get the hell up!* Glancing down at his hands, he grimaced as blood dripped from his fingers to splash into a dark red puddle at his feet.

Get it together, Garcia. Stand to attention. Now!

Breathe. He needed to breathe. Dragging in oxygen, he infused his spine with steel and reached for the plateau between consciousness and serenity. In and out, slow and even. His mind's eyes gradually turned black, his heartbeat slowed, and a voice filtered through the murky haze.

'…and then the brave dark knight took out his sword and fought the dragon with all his might. Past the castle walls, past fire and flame, through the walls of men he charged to find her. Up the stairs to the turret where she lay in a deep sleep waiting for his kiss…'

Claudia?

His eyes sprang open and Lucas scanned the hallway for the direction of her voice, moved stealthily towards an open door.

'Oh, and she was so beautiful. With long golden hair, just

like yours, and big blue eyes the colour of the Arunthian ocean…'

'Like mine?' a little voice asked.

'Just like yours.'

'No one would want to kiss *me,*' came the little voice.

'Oh, the dark knight would want a kiss. But you'd have to be older. Like the Princess. And when you're older your eyes won't be sore any more and your wrists will be just like mine. See?'

Lucas surveyed the small room, knowing he shouldn't be intruding—that it was, as Claudia had said, private. And Bailey sounded very much like a young girl. Not a man. The rapid flush of relief was because she was safe, he was sure.

Claudia was perched on the edge of a small bed, blocking his view of the patient. Her jacket was gone, the sleeves of her shirt rolled high as she twisted her arm this way and that, seemingly allowing the girl to inspect her wrists. He remembered all the times she'd tugged at her clothes, and earlier when he'd grabbed her.

Stiffening his limbs, he fought the emotional throb of his body.

'I wouldn't want to kiss a boy anyway,' Bailey said. 'Clara in Bay Four said it's like eating custard. I hate custard.'

'Custard?' Claudia repeated, and Lucas could hear the smile in her voice. He wished she wasn't turned away from him so he could see the widening of her lush mouth for himself.

'But maybe my dad would come…'

'I know, darling,' Claudia said softly, the affection in her voice strong, the rich, melodic tone unfamiliar to him. Yet somehow it had the power to unearth a long-buried memory and create a strange surge of longing. 'I know,' she repeated. 'Look what I brought for you.'

Claudia bent from the waist, reaching into her bag on the floor, and his attention snapped to the child. *Dios…*

He stepped to the side in an instant, before she caught sight of him, unwilling to frighten her. His size tended to do just that and she was immensely frail. *Frail?* She was tiny.

'Who's that man, Claudia?' the girl asked.

Damn. Lucas schooled his features, flexed his neck and relaxed his big body in an attempt to become as unthreatening as he possibly could. Then he turned to the open doorway, almost filling the narrow gap.

'Good morning,' he said.

The girl, Bailey, gaped openly, and Claudia shot to her feet. 'Lucas. What are you doing here? Can't I have one hour's peace?'

'Sí,' he said. 'Except it now happens to be one hour and twenty-three minutes.' He turned to Bailey. 'May I come in?'

'No,' Claudia said.

'Okay,' Bailey said.

'Since this is your room, *señorita,* I shall take your answer,' he said to the young girl, and was rewarded with a small tentative smile. One that lifted the heavy bruising from around her eyes and sent a fresh burst of emotion through his system.

Claudia fisted her small hands as if she wanted to punch him into next week, and stepped toward the bed in an entirely protective move. What the hell did she think he would do?

As he approached the bed Claudia moved closer still, practically smothering his view. And, like a warning flare illuminating the sky, light dawned. She was not only protecting the child, she was *hiding* her.

He tossed Claudia a quizzical look and she volleyed with a silent plea, mouthed, 'Do not stare.'

Anger screamed through his innards, blending with affront, and he ground his jaw fiercely to prevent it pouring from his mouth. He'd always prided himself on being unreadable—he'd been trained by the best, after all—but the chastised look on Claudia's face told him he'd failed to hide his fury in this instance. And he was inordinately pleased.

In one sweeping glance he'd gained several key pieces that made up the Princess Claudine Verbault conundrum. *And when you're older...your wrists will be just like mine...*she'd said. This girl had the same condition that Claudia had suffered from in her youth. Lucas was looking at the past.

At enflamed wrists and elbows, painfully sore skin. At puffy eyes and purplish branding that spoke of bone-deep lethargy. And the way she barely moved from the bed, wincing as she tried to straighten her legs, told him she suffered serious muscle fatigue. Tiny hands tugged at the white sheet to drape over her slight frame. Hiding.

Pain banked in his chest. Through it all, the girl was very pretty, and he could see glimpses of the beautiful woman she would become. A woman who would replace the white sheet with a dour wardrobe.

Madre de Dios. His gut ached.

While he'd read brief notes on the illness, seeing it, looking at it for himself, was something else entirely. Much like visiting a bombsite—knowing the damage was already done, hoping for the best, but witnessing devastation that left soldiers numb for hours.

Clearing his thick, tight throat, he looked towards Claudia. 'Would you like to make the introductions?'

Her deep amber eyes bored through his skull and he returned her glare, caught in that odd battle of wills that so often ensnared them. Not once had he lost the fight, and this time the stakes were gravely higher.

Soon enough she blinked, then stepped to the side. 'Bailey, this is Lucas. Lucas, this is my friend Bailey.'

Lucas tore his gaze from Claudia, knowing full well that he shouldn't be here. That with every passing second he was becoming more embroiled with the mysterious Arunthian Princess. It wasn't his job to consider her past, present or her future. Getting her home was his remit. His obligation. His mission. His promise to the King.

Pausing for a second, he weighed the risk. Looked at the expectant child, the hopeful softening of Claudia's beautiful face.

'*Buenos días,* Bailey,' he said, with a quick bow that pinked her cheeks. 'I am honoured to meet you.'

* * *

Claudia tried to pick her jaw up off the floor and only just managed when Lucas raised one dark brow in her direction. Clearly he had no idea of the in-topics for girly conversation, because small talk slipped in a steady decline and he kept looking to Claudia for direction. And each time he did something warm and delicious unfurled inside her.

Oh, God, he was utterly wonderful. Which was great for Bailey, disastrous for her. She wanted to hate him. For barging into her life, stripping away her independence. For taking her away from Bailey and throwing her to the wolves.

He was the oddest mixture of man. Arrogant. Infuriating. Thoughtful.

'We have to leave now, Bailey,' she said, her heart breaking in two. 'I won't be able to visit for a few weeks, but I'll be back.'

Claudia stared into her big blue eyes, willing her to believe. Because she knew exactly how she felt. One sentence—*I'll be back*—had the power to plague you with excitement for hours and then crush your heart when no one came.

Bailey tried for a smile and Claudia's throat stung under a seething fire.

'I'll be back. I promise,' Claudia said, making a cross on her breast with the tip of her finger. 'And I'll bring you a present. The most beautiful gift you've ever seen. And I'll write,' she said, her voice laced with desperation, her hands trembling, her chest quaking. 'We can e-mail, just like I showed you.'

Claudia grabbed her jacket from the back of the chair, silently chanting. *Three weeks. Then you'll have the money to finish what you started. You'll be back to hold her hand every day. Just three weeks.*

Blinded by the need for air, Claudia stormed down the hall and stopped dead at the double doors leading to the stairwell, opposite the gaping steel mouth of the lift. Seven flights of stairs might be nothing to Action-Man, but she didn't have a hope of making them.

'Claudia?'

'Don't speak. Don't be nice, please.' She'd break. She'd crumble. And no way was she doing that in front of this man.

Lucas eyed the steel box with something close to contempt and Claudia laughed. The hollow sound echoed off the green-flecked walls. He couldn't even bear to get in the lift with her. And, my God, it hurt. Why did she persecute herself like this? Wishing, dreaming of things she could never have.

Turning, palms flat, she pushed through the double doors and begged her legs to stay strong, keep her upright.

'Claudia, slow down.'

Step, step, step went her feet. The heavy thud of Lucas came behind her. Bearing upon her. Closing in. 'Where do you get off, telling me what to do?' she muttered, her breath short and raspy, her feet now pounding down the stairs.

'Claudia, I understand—'

His voice verged on the consoling, and the hint of pity unleashed the storm raging inside her. 'You had no right. No right coming up there!'

'We are on a strict time limit,' he said harshly, while the thud, thud of his shoes became louder, echoing off the walls and drubbing her temples.

Don't you dare fall, Claudia. Don't you dare.

'Oh, please,' she said. 'You've just wasted twenty minutes talking. If…if time was so important to you…you would've ordered me out of that room instantly.'

'*Dios,* Claudia, slow down. You will fall. I realise you are anxious—'

'Anxious?' she said, stumbling when the first flight broke for a landing and a human blur jumped from the sky and landed dead in front of her. *Too close. Too close.* Taking a step back, she winced as pain shot up her calf and continued to vent, 'Do you know how many people will visit her while I'm gone? *Do* you?'

He said nothing, just looked at her with a grim expression that made her feel even worse. For God's sake, he wasn't even breathing hard. While she rasped and heaved as if she'd endured a triathlon.

'Her mother died when Bailey fell ill and her father works on an oil rig. If she's lucky he'll come by once during his leave.' More family visits than Claudia had ever had, but that was between her and her parents. 'But why am I telling you this, Lucas? I forgot. You don't feel, right? How can you possibly know what I feel like right now?'

Her back slapped against the wall but this time he kept his distance. Though from the lines scoring his handsome face it seemed to cost him.

'I do not. But I can see leaving her torments you. So many things make sense to me now, but you will be back. You have other responsibilities, Claudia.'

'Oh, Lucas, shove your royal responsibilities where the sun doesn't shine, will you?'

He massaged the bridge of his nose with his thumb and forefinger. He did that a lot, she realised.

'So elegant. So refined.'

'What are you? My elocutionist? I had one of those once. The woman lasted three days.'

'I am not surprised. I imagine you scared her off.'

'Probably. *You* try being a European princess dropped in a London hospital and surrounded by children who talk of apples and pears when all you want to know is where the stairs are.'

He frowned. 'Apples?'

'And pears. So, you see, her version of helping was a bit like yours. Unwanted.'

Frightened, alone, she'd been drowning in a river of intolerance, bitterness towards the elite, so she'd done the only thing she could to survive. Shunned her aristocratic birthright. Not that she'd cared. She would have done anything to forget who she truly was. And now they wanted her back. A woman who didn't exist.

'You are hurting. If it makes you feel any better hit me. Hard. But *do not* give up. Courage, Claudia.'

Closing the gap, he reached up and brushed the hair from her brow, the slight scrape making her shiver. She had no idea what possessed her. Maybe it was the sympathy in his eyes— God, she hated that. But she hit him. Just once. Her small fist connected to his shoulder with a soft thump. Not even hard. Her heart wasn't in it, she realised. It was too busy breaking.

Throat stinging, eyes shuttering, her legs gave way. And he was there, scooping her into his arms, lifting her close, laying her against his broad, muscular chest and walking down the stairs as if she weighed nothing more than a test strip. And in that moment she'd never despised herself more.

Twisting, she pushed against his chest. 'Put me down. I don't need you to carry me.' She didn't need anyone. Least of all him.

'Be still.' His bark reverberated off the walls. 'And in future I suggest you give more thought to your body than your pride and take the lift when your legs ache.'

'What are you? A telepath?' The fight slowly drained from her body. 'God, I hate you right now,' she whispered, even as she laid her head against his carved shoulder. He was so strong…so annoying…so everything.

'*Bueno*. That is good,' he said, his voice dropping to a low, somewhat soothing husky rumble.

As he embraced her so tightly Claudia tried to remember if anyone had ever held her close. No. Never. Not even when she was a little girl. And it felt…wonderful.

Her body grew lax, her breathing steadied and his luxurious sandalwood scent enveloped her in a cashmere blanket. His heart thumped beneath her cheek, lulling. Claudia wrapped her arms about his neck, snuggled against him, burrowing, suddenly desperate to absorb his strength. Had she ever felt so safe in her life? It would be oh-so-easy to need him. And oh-so-stupid even to contemplate it.

On instinct she brushed her nose up the column of his throat to his unyielding jaw, the rasp of morning growth tickling the tip. A shiver racked through her core, so addictive she did it again. Blood rushed through her head, drowning out sound, but she felt his chest rumble in a little quake before he swayed slightly on his feet.

'Claudia,' he said, his voice tight, throaty, as if he needed a drink.

She needed something, but water was the last thing on her mind. She felt extraordinary. An incredible blend of fizzy excitement and drugging anxiousness.

Summoning the courage to lift her head, she looked up, felt his breath trickle over her face, so close. Her mouth was mere inches away from his lips. 'Lucas?'

He had a mystifying glint in his eyes, pupils dilated, heavy. Hot. 'Do not do that, Claudia. I cannot—'

'Why not?' she whispered, moving a little closer…

Then *leap* went her heart when, in one deft move, he sank his fingers beneath the loose twist at her nape and whisked his arm from under her thighs until she slid down his hard body onto her feet. With his free hand he brushed a stray curl from her eyes so she could see him properly, or maybe so *he* could see all of her. And all the while his fingers tightened in her hair, sending tides of sensation flooding down her spine in one glorious wave after another.

'So brave,' he said, eyes glittering like two rare sapphires.

Was it pity she could see lurking in the depths? *Please, no*—anything but that.

His body grew as taut as his jaw and she fancied he fought some inner battle. One she lost when he slackened his hold, sending her stomach plunging to the floor. *No.* Claudia grabbed a handful of his shirt to stay upright, to bring him back…

A groan tore up his throat and with one tug—*oh, yes*—his mouth was on hers. Soft, yet achingly hard, scorching her lips until she burst into flames.

Alive. She'd never felt so alive. Her entire body shook with an excitement so intense it blanked all thought of self-preservation.

His kiss was blatant and intense as he bowed her in a delicate arch, caged by the unyielding steel frame of his awesome body. Firm, smooth lips moved over hers, back and forth so skilfully she quickly cottoned on to his rhythm and skill, earning a wickedly thrilling growl. The touch of his tongue sliding against her lower lip, flicking to the corner, was a call to surrender and she opened for him with a high-pitched moan, laying siege to his delicious assault.

Eyes closed, fingers flaring on his shoulders, she plastered herself against him. The crush of her heavy breasts, the flick of his velvet tongue against hers, set off a chemical reaction: heat surged through her veins, the deafening rush of blood sped past her ears. A hot splash of liquid melted her core—awakening her body in a way she'd never dreamed of. Never known existed. And all she could think was more, *more.*

Her fingers skimmed the broad contours of his shoulders, followed the column of his neck and slid under his ears…into his hair.

Lucas groaned long and low, tightening his hold, one hand on her nape, the other still at her waist, until she felt precious, wanted.

Desired.

The seductive pull of his mouth became pure exhilaration as she felt his hands wander, as if he craved to learn her shape—curving over her hips, slinking into her waist. And when his thumbs brushed the underside of her breasts…*oh, my.*

No fantasy had ever lived up to this. Even when she'd lain in bed the previous night, knowing Lucas was so close in the room next door, dreaming he'd kiss her awake, imagining the hard press of his weight on top of her.

As if caught in between a dream and reality she ground her pelvis against him—instinctive, wanting—and revelled in the thick hard ridge digging into her stomach. The thought of that part of him inside her drove a soft pleading moan past her lips.

Lucas stilled, his mouth fused with hers. His breath, warm and wet, slipped past her parted lips. 'Claudia?' Gruff, yet undoubtedly perturbed, his voice doused the flames of desire and she rocked back on her heels.

'*Dios,*' he muttered, scooping her back up against his chest. 'I need to get you out of here.'

She said nothing, just buried her hot face in his shoulder, trying not to touch, twisting her fingers together in the deep well between her stomach and his. Her brain was in a complete state of confusion. Why had he kissed her? What on earth had possessed her to kiss *him?* One minute she'd been ranting like some despicable idiot and the next... Heart breaking, she'd craved a distraction—that was all. Maybe comfort. There wasn't anything pathetic about that, was there?

Oh, God.

Any lingering warmth froze solid in her veins as he opened the door and reality closed in.

Daylight stroked her eyelids. London's midday crush filtered through her ears and Lucas's scent was replaced with smoggy car fumes and greasy bacon from the van permanently stationed in the hospital car park. The mingling aromas were enough to plunge her farther into reality, and her heart crumpled when she realised what she'd allowed Lucas to see. Her. Pathetic and needy. Vulnerable. The girl she'd buried long ago.

'Are you able to stand?' he asked.

'Of course,' she said, sliding down his body to her feet. The sensation reminded her, made her voice hitch. 'Thank you.'

He raked an irritable hand round the back of his neck. 'Claudia, about what just happened...'

He averted his gaze to some place over her left shoulder. But not before she caught the glimpse of uneasy regret.

Claudia closed her eyes. It was worse than she'd thought.

Sharing a student flat at university had taught her to close her ears to wanton chatter. But she wasn't tone deaf or completely ignorant about sex. She'd heard of a pity lay, and she guessed she'd just experienced the pity-kiss equivalent. The thought made her feel physically sick. Yes, she'd felt him, hard and amazing against her stomach, but how many times had she seen classmates hop from one bed to another regardless of attraction? Sex was sex to men, as long as it resulted in a high-octane pay-off.

'I should not have done it,' he bit out, anger slashing across his cheeks.

'You're right. You shouldn't. Not for the reasons you did.'

His brow crunched, his mouth shaping for speech, and she couldn't bear to hear any more excuses. This was humiliating enough.

'Don't worry about it, Lucas. It meant nothing, right?' She shrugged in an attempt to lighten the mood.

'Right.'

'We'll just go on like it never happened.'

Painfully aware he was starting to read her like a kindergarten book, she didn't appreciate the way he scanned her face. The notion made her reach for a curveball and throw it out there. 'I just thought—what the hell? I'll try it.'

A stunned light flashed in his intense stare. *'Qué?'*

'Kissing,' she said, her heart lifting as she warmed to the idea. The *last* thing she needed was Lucas thinking she had designs on him. 'It was better than I thought.'

He blinked.

She smiled.

'That,' he said, pointing back to the hospital, still blinking wide eyes, 'was the first time you've been…*kissed?*'

'Yes.'

It took a few seconds for him to absorb that tasty little snippit, his jaw falling off its hinges in the process. As embarrassing as never-been-kissed was to admit, it was a far better alternative to the undoubted ego-boost that she fancied the pants off him.

And then her scurrilous mind darted in yet another direction, spawning her need to be the very best. At everything.

'So tell me, just so I know for the future, did I do it right?'

A sound spluttered from his lips—something between a cough and a growl. *'Sí,'* he said vaguely. Too vaguely for her liking.

He was just being a gentleman. She didn't like being under par. As a person she fed off success. On an intellectual level, that was. Until now.

She rubbed her fingertips across the plump flesh of her lips. Had she been too soft? Too hard? Too wet? Maybe she hadn't opened her mouth enough. It had been perfectly delicious to her, but…

Oh, heavens. He was staring at her mouth.

She stilled.

His eyes shot up to hers: liquid ozone, dark and intense. 'And was it as you'd hoped?'

Stifling a smile, she went for light, airy. 'Oh, it was fine. Nothing like custard.'

CHAPTER SIX

NEVER BEEN KISSED.

Lucas sat in the plush lounge area of the jet, coffee sliding over his tongue, scorching the erotic blend of Claudia from his mouth. Lowering the cup to the table, he glanced covertly across the cabin to where she'd finally settled—curled into a deep swivel bucket seat, her long legs dangling over the side.

She was buried in work. Fierce concentration marred the silky skin of her brow as she pushed her glasses up her nose and scribbled another note in her book.

Did I do it right?

Lucas scrubbed his hands over his face. Trust Claudia to pour every ounce of delectable effort into her first kiss and succeed in blowing his mind.

What the hell had he been thinking, kissing her in the first place? He hadn't been thinking. Not with the correct head anyway. With one forbidden touch he'd lost control. *Dios,* he should never have laid a finger on her. But she'd been aching, hurting. The pain in her eyes had thrown him.

Practically across the corridor.

Holding her—her scent a warm shroud, her flesh heating his blood, her touch a sensual deluge—resistance had become futile.

And if he thought Claudia had been lost in the moment she'd soon murdered the notion, squashing his ego like a bug underfoot. No, no, *no*—she'd just wanted to *try* it! *Madre de*

Dios, what was he? One of her experiments? And his kiss apparently was *fine.* She'd used the most insipid word in the universe. To describe him. While he'd sunk deeper into the abyss with every tentative stroke of her tongue.

If one kiss could devour his body and mind, what kind of destruction could she cause with her clothes off? He was a man who preferred a predictable low-level and controllable response to a woman. Yet he was hard just thinking about sinking into her sensational body—as ludicrous and impossible as it was.

Jacket discarded, she still wore the fawn silk shirt and figure-hugging trousers of earlier, and he swallowed around a bullet-clogged barrel. His hands were imprinted with her flesh, firm and lush, and his eyes dipped to her breasts, remembering the heavy weight of their perfection.

Catching a groan halfway up his throat, Lucas tore his eyes away, tension building in his chest as he became more resentful of her powerful allure. Not only was she his current mission, he lived his life free of encumbrance and always would. To be in thrall to his desires, to any kind of emotion, was like begging for an assassin's bullet: it made you weak. So he worked, he fought for everything he believed in—justice, honour, duty— the only way he knew how. Hollow to the core.

Claudia—any woman, for that matter—deserved far more than an empty shell of a man.

Lost in thought, he mechanically ate lunch. Claudia declined anything bar a glass of sparkling water, and the silence stretched to breaking point.

Until the smack and skid of a glossy magazine on the table in front of him broke through the lull.

'What…?' She took a deep breath. 'What is this, Lucas?'

Hands flat to the table, Claudia leaned forward, and he ordered his eyes not to dip to the gaping V of her shirt and the heaving swell of smooth golden skin. Skin he could kiss and lick and suck for hours, until the woman forgot her own name and begged him to—

'A magazine,' he said, as fierce as the erection pushing against his zipper.

'Funny how you've never bothered to tell me the real reason my parents want me back.'

He shifted slightly, grateful for the mention of her parents. His promise. Her duty. 'They wish to see you. That is the true reason.'

'No. They want to showcase their perfect family to the world for the event of the decade.' Her trembling fingers curled into fists in front of him, and a quiver seeped through her voice. 'A party, Lucas?'

'What is so bad about a party?'

'They want a princess and I'm no longer that person. I can't be what they want. You told me—'

'You can be anyone you want to be. I have seen enough versions of Claudia in the past twenty-four hours to convince me of that.'

The ice maiden, the seductive intellectual, a Mother Teresa, and glimpses of a vulnerability that cut him to the core. Not forgetting the scientist who wanted scoring on a kiss. *Dios,* little wonder he didn't know what he was about in her company. She did *not* make sense.

His stomach dipped in time with the plane. 'Buckle up, Princess.'

She scrambled onto the seat beside him, her fraying temper visibly morphing into sheer panic. 'Could we circle a few more times?'

Her fingers fumbled with the metal buckle and after a few seconds he pushed her hands away and clicked it shut.

'No, we cannot. What is wrong with you?'

Amber eyes locked on his. 'I'm not too good with people.'

'*Qué?* Do I look stupid to you, Claudia? Within ten minutes of our meeting you were chewing my head off, and you were perfectly at ease with Armande and Bailey.'

'I've known Bailey for months. She's a child. And how

would you know how I was with Armande? You left me! So much for your personal protection.'

Indignity was a slap in his face. 'I was dealing with the rep—' He broke off. She didn't need to know about the reporter. He still had a hard time believing he could have been so negligent. This was what she did to him. Threw him so far off course it was like navigating the jungle without a compass.

'Reporter?' Her hand curled up her chest to wrap around her throat, where her pulse beat erratically. 'The man outside my flat? You found him?'

'*Sí*. Not a figment of my imagination after all.'

She sucked her bottom lip into her mouth. 'Did he take pictures?'

'Yes. I destroyed them.'

Her eyes turned stormy, frantic. 'This is what it's going to be like. I'm going to be watched. Stared at. Photographed. Basically put under the microscope.' Her words trailed to a panicked whisper.

A coil of unease snaked through his guts. *That* was the problem, he realised. Without camouflage, with her identity known, she couldn't hide. Neither from the paparazzi nor in a ballroom full to bursting with people.

Bracing himself for landing, he waited for the inevitable crash.

'I can't do it, Lucas. I'm sorry,' she said, shaking her head, her amber eyes brimming with tears. Tears that tore at his heart. 'You have to turn this plane around and take me home.'

Lucas rejected the imminent threat of a memory ready to suck him under. 'Impossible. I cannot. It is too late.'

He had to get her home. Her true home. Not some dingy flat in central London. She needed to be with her family, surrounded by the dense, protective barrier of the palace walls. Where she could finally do her duty and take responsibility for that part of her life.

Long fingers gripped his forearm, bit into his flesh, frenzied…wild. 'You can do anything you want to, Lucas. I know that now.'

'No, I—' He broke off, steely dread making his limbs feel heavy as he sank down, down, suffocating under the sudden image of another time, another place, another woman. Begging him to hide her, desperate fear in her eyes for what was to come.

A woman who hid from the world while vulnerability ruled her every waking moment.

The truth slammed into him.

This was the real Claudia Verbault. She too hid her tender vulnerabilities, her secrets from the world—just as his mother had. A woman who'd needed him. A woman he'd failed.

'Please. I'm begging you, Lucas. Take me home.'

Claudia was way past the point of no return. Lucas had been so distracting she'd never even given herself time to consider what arriving in Arunthia would feel like. Now she knew. It felt as if the world was about to quake, slash open to form a gigantic crater and swallow her whole.

Buried deep, her memories began to scramble to the surface, hitting her with one deft punch after another.

It was quite possible that at the back of her mind she'd hoped her parents wanted to see her again so desperately they would do anything. Like send a towering brute to give her three and a half million pounds to make her happy. She was such a fool. They wanted Claudine the Princess, and she was anything but. She wasn't ready. Nowhere near ready. She wanted to go home and wrap herself in a warm cocoon. To think of work— the only thing she knew, the only thing she was good at. To be alone and safe. Just for a little while longer.

The ache in her stomach was another deep, dark hollow that seemed to engulf her very soul.

Yes, Lucas had been right about the reporter, and from the look on his face there was more to that story than he was telling her. Were people so interested in her? *Please, no.* She couldn't cope with that kind of intrusion.

Lucas was staring at her, thunderclouds brewing in his dark eyes. Then he blinked and vanquished the storm. '*Dios,* you are trembling. Claudia, all will be well. Your family will be there for you.'

A mirthless laugh burst from her searing throat. Her parents offering her *support?* 'Oh, Lucas, you have no idea.'

He frowned. 'So tell me.'

How could she? He worked for the crown. She could sense he respected her parents. Admired them. And deep down she knew Lucas would take their side. She might as well dig compassion out of a stone.

'I've been away from here so long,' she said, trying to think of a way to explain past the insistent throb in her head.

Smack went the wheels against the tarmac and Claudia rocked back in her seat. *Oh, God. Think, Claudia, think.*

The wings kicked up, the jet slowed and horror stung the back of her retinas at the sight before her. 'Oh, no.' She gripped his arm tighter, her fingertips digging through dense muscle. Hordes. What looked like thousands of flesh-eaters, hauling huge great cameras. Ready to pounce. 'No photographs.'

Lucas glanced at the pack, seemingly unaffected. While she felt wild, miserable, attacked.

'I can't do this. I'm sorry. Truly. Blame everything on me. Tell them I'm selfish and unreasonable and you tried everything.'

Cupping her face, Lucas looked into her eyes. 'Calm yourself. A car will pull up at the bottom of the steps. Let them see the beautiful Princess has returned home. Hold your head high.'

'No. They'll follow us…' She blinked at a flash. A memory. A noose wrapped around her heart tugged, choking the life out of her. How had she forgotten about that? 'Like before…' The car. The plink and flash of cameras. Her mother. The screaming. 'I think I'm going to throw up.'

His expression grew dark and as taut as the fingers cradling her face. 'Before?'

Throat burning, she gave a little shake of her head. Unwilling, unable to go back, revisit.

After a few beats he sighed. 'They cannot pass the enclosure. We will not be followed.' His voice turned fierce, indomitable. 'I promise you. I am here. You are safe. I will not let anything happen to you.'

Claudia closed her eyes. God, she wanted his lips on hers. He made her forget everything. Lucas made her feel safe.

Her eyes snapped open. 'And what happens when you drop me off at the palace and leave me there?'

Hands sliding from her cheeks, his gaze drifted to some place over her right shoulder. So strange that he was still right in front of her and yet it was as if he'd physically left. Leaving a numb sensation climbing up her spine. Because wasn't that always the way?

'You will have the best guards,' he said, his powerful voice blazing with conviction, an oath written in blood. 'I swear it.'

Everything inside her rebelled. 'No. I want you. Only you. *You* brought me here.' And he could damn well stick with her.

Reticence engulfed him, sharpening the air. 'Very well,' he said, his hand fisting against the tabletop as if the very idea was anathema to him. 'I will be in charge of your full security.' His gaze flicked back to hers. 'Yes?'

She slouched back into her seat. 'Yes. Okay. I'll stay with you.'

'What?' he said, his thunderous voice caroming around the cabin.

'That's the deal. Surely you have a house…a spare room?'

'You cannot be serious!'

'Deadly,' she said, switching off her pride button—a surprisingly easy feat when she considered the alternative. 'You take me with you or you turn this plane around.'

'*Dios,* Claudia, it is not appropriate. Have you lost your

mind?' he asked, incredulity contorting his features as if he was staring at a scary mad person.

It was a look that made her falter. *Was* she crazy? To ask for shelter under his roof. Yearning for his touch the way she did?

But after four hours cooped up on a plane she'd had time to put their kiss to rest. Clearly Lucas wasn't interested, and in three weeks she would have her life back. That was all she wanted. Her freedom. Until then she needed to feel safe. And, without knowing how or why, she trusted him with her life.

'We've just spent the last two days together,' she said. 'Was that appropriate?'

'*Sí.* We were in a different country. And your father expects you at the palace.'

'Just tell him I'm awkward and selfish and I need a little time. Nothing but the truth. Right?'

'Right.'

His eyes plummeted to her mouth and she watched them ignite, flare into a sapphire blaze. An answering heat unfurled deep down in her core even as she told herself he was simply vexed with her.

His words, the way he ground them out, confirmed her suspicions. 'The answer is still no. What you ask is impossible.'

Claudia lurched as the jet came to a dead stop. Reeled at the sight of a world long forgotten. Glanced at the harsh Mediterranean sun bouncing off the asphalt. Grappled with her shirtsleeves, pulling at the soft silk, desperate to be covered. 'What you asked of me yesterday morning was impossible in my mind, Lucas,' she said, the pit of despair gaping wider. 'Yet here I am. So, you see, nothing is impossible.'

From the corner of her eye she watched him flex his neck, his wide chest heave.

'We cannot always have what we desire, Claudia,' he bit out.

'Fine.' She pinned her spine to the seat and pulled the cord on her belt to cinch the black strap nice and tight. 'Refuel and take me home. Your mission is unaccomplished. Because I'm not getting off this plane.'

He raked his hands through his gorgeous sable hair and the silence stretched to a thick oppression. One she couldn't seem to breathe through.

One of the male flight attendants swerved towards them and Lucas hollered, 'Go the hell away.' So loud Claudia flinched.

Waiting until the attendant had darted towards the cockpit and disappeared from sight, she turned back to Lucas. 'Are you angry with me?' Stupid question when she was hyper-aware of the dark power emanating from his body, pulsing through the air, humming over her skin. Perversely, she'd never felt so protected in her entire life.

'Goddamn furious. You play a dangerous game with me, Claudia. I make the rules. *Comprende?*'

Oh, she understood perfectly. 'So tell me the new rules and I'll obey. Every single one.'

CHAPTER SEVEN

'Wow. Being Head of Security must pay well.'

With the exception of Marianne, his housekeeper, Lucas had never had a woman in his home before. Now he knew why. It was a complete invasion of privacy and entirely too distracting. He'd rather camp with twenty men than one of Claudia.

'Glass. Everywhere. I suddenly feel like a goldfish swimming around an enormous bowl,' she said, with a quick tug on the sleeves of her jacket.

Ah, yes, Lucas mused, his mouth twisting. She preferred walls of steel to match the walls she'd built up inside herself. At first he'd thought the vulnerability was her cloak. He'd been wrong. It was her inner core. Everything was designed to fight off intruders like some high-tech alarm system. Together with her high intellect, it was unsurprising no one had managed to breach it.

Standing in the centre of the hundred-foot open-plan living area, he watched her absorb his life, the pit of his stomach weighted with lead. This was a mistake. He knew it. He didn't want her here. Didn't want any woman here. Especially not her. But what choice did he have? Dragging her to the palace would have been more barbaric than even he was capable of. And the panic, the terror, the vulnerability in her eyes—*Dios,* it got to him every time. At least here she was safe. From what haunting demons he had no idea. But he intended to find out.

'The view is the most spectacular I've ever seen,' she said, awe lending her voice a creamy note. She moved up close to the wide plate glass, looking towards the ocean, and sunlight gilded her in an angelic aura. He knew then she'd been in the dark too long.

She trailed her fingers along the polished black top of his baby grand and he could feel those very tips branding his skin, setting his blood on fire.

'I'm not sure what I expected,' she said, slowing to examine an original masterpiece taking centre stage on one of the few internal walls. 'Beautiful brush strokes. I'm sure the National Gallery has one of these.'

With a tilt of her head she bestowed upon him her profile. The soft curve of her lip told him she knew all too well the value of the painting. But purchasing the portrait hadn't been about money or investment or even the artist. It had everything to do with the subject.

'What did you expect?' he asked, unsure why he even cared for her opinion.

Swivelling on her low heels to face him, she gave a small smile, lifted at one side in a kind of embarrassment. 'Probably some Americanised version of a bachelor pad. Huge TV, empty pizza boxes and…' Colour warmed her cheeks rose-gold.

'And?'

'I was going to say a stash of *Playboy* magazines, but for all I know you have a girlfriend.' Biting her lip, she lifted one foot, bent her ankle and scratched her opposite calf with the black peeptoe. 'Which, come to think of it, is something I should've asked before I ki—'

Jumping in before the image engulfed him, he bit out, 'I do not get involved with women, Claudia.' He laid his commitment-free card face-up. For both their sakes. Lucas would *not* kiss her under this roof. Because if he did he would never stop.

Claudia pursed her lips, canted her head. 'At all?'

'No. Like you, I live for my work. I have neither the time nor the inclination for relationships.'

He had one-hour-stands with women who knew the rules.

Claudia wouldn't know what to do with a rulebook if it smacked her on the head—something that made him doubly wary of their current predicament.

'Something else we have in common, then,' she said.

'I cannot think of any possible "something else".'

'You value your privacy. You don't talk much about yourself.'

'It is not necessary in my job.' He was being sharp—overly so. But he needed her to understand. Just because she'd managed to wrangle herself a bed under his roof it didn't mean she could burrow into his life. And to stop her from doing just that, Lucas was determined to focus on hers. When she finally decamped he'd make damn sure she held her head high, without the need for any of her façades.

'Our agreement was one week. Seven days and seven nights you may stay. Your father was quite willing to allow you time to acclimatise.' The relief in Henri's voice had said it all. She was on Arunthian soil and that was what mattered. Lucas's secluded estate rivalled Fort Knox, so they would be free from prying eyes.

No, the real problem was standing directly in front of him. One finger swirling around her pout, one hip tilted in that sexy pose that made his blood roar. *Dios*...

Hoping she would retire and leave him with some measure of peace, he said, 'First thing tomorrow we visit your parents, and during the remaining time I will reintroduce you to your country.'

Eyes widening, her mouth worked. 'Tomorrow?'

'*Sí*. And then I will show you your *real* home.' Once she became captivated by her heritage and discerned her true import the desire to do her duty would come, he was sure.

If what she said was true and she was uncomfortable around people he needed to fix it. Otherwise, come the end of the week, they would be back to square one and there was no way she could stay here for *three* weeks. He would go grey. And insane. The sooner she was confident in her abilities the sooner she would be gone from his life.

Gone. Ignoring the sharp blade driving through his gut, he forged on. He had to tear down her defences one by one, vanquish every fear. It was his job, he told himself, despite the claw at his conscience saying otherwise.

'Firstly, do *not* concern yourself with the paparazzi or your personal safety. There was a time when Arunthia was plagued with villainy and the crime rate was high. Too high,' he said, keeping his voice steady, betraying none of the emotion warring inside. 'But not any more.'

Dark brows rose above stunned amber eyes. 'Not since you took over, you mean?'

'*Exactamente.* Welcome home, *Just Claudia.*'

The *whoop, whoop* of rotorblades echoed the thump of her anxious heart as they flew over the famed hunting grounds of her childhood residence. And when Arunthe Palace burst into view—standing atop a gigantic rock in dramatic cliff-edge splendour—it was as if the helicopter had been torn open beneath her feet and she was freefalling to earth.

Cream stone-walls, fanciful turrets with conical slate roofs, large spiralling towers firing into the sky like fireworks—a Disney-esque vision that was merely an illusion, a fairytale. For no happy endings could arise from this world of chilling austerity.

Despite all the years of fighting for her freedom she was finally here. Her parents had sent King Kong for Fay Wray and she'd never had a chance. And some sixth sense ran like a river of screams beneath her skin, warning her that now she'd returned she would never escape. *Nonsense, Claudia. Breathe.*

The military helicoptor touched down and she ordered her legs to stand tall, stay strong, even as she reached for her iron mask, admitting, if only to herself, that she would have done anything for Lucas to take her hand and hold it tightly in his.

So she could absorb his awesome strength. *No, Claudia. Self-reliant. Always self-reliant.*

By the time they were ushered into her mother's apartment, her stomach was alive with seething nausea, and the sickly scent of lavender hit her just as hard as the sight of Marysse Verbault.

Dressed in an elegant buttery skirt suit and a black chiffon blouse, with not one hair escaping her coiffed dark pleat, she oozed class and sophistication. Claudia pinched her fingers to stop herself from smoothing her own rumpled *'dour'* appearance or tugging on the threadbare hem of her sleeve.

Then that voice—so cool, so calm—stroked her soul with fingers of ice. 'Claudine. Finally. Let me look at you.'

A bolt of indignation shot down her spine and pinned her in place. At one time this woman hadn't been able to bear to look at her. To touch her. Yet now her mother clasped her upper arms and Claudia foraged for the bravura to lock onto the amber eyes that were so like her own. Not only that, for one cataclysmic beat of her heart Claudia imagined her mother wanted to embrace her, and one tiny part of her—the little girl she had once been—wanted that so much. Craved to know she was wanted for herself, loved in some small way. But her mother merely examined every inch of her face, as if to check her daughter was well—well enough to parade in front of thousands.

'I am very happy to see to you, Claudine. Look, Henri, our daughter is finally home.'

Resisting the urge to argue that *London* was her home, she waited for his words…then flinched when his imperious voice caromed around the room.

'It is about time. Good job, Lucas.'

Claudia perfected a smile that cracked her heart and looked across the opulent expanse of the room to where Henri Verbault stood with Lucas in front of a large, ornate cherrywood desk, papers in hand. Age had amplified his autocratic demeanour even as his greying hair softened the contours of his face.

'Good morning, Father.'

'*Buenos días,* Claudine.' Steel-grey determined eyes held hers, turning liquid with something like relief. Relief that she was well, or relief that she was back to pay her dues? Who knew? He turned his attention back to Lucas, her dismissal loud and true.

'Sit down. Take tea.'

Her mother's voice warmed just a touch as she perched on the edge of a Gustavian carver chair, one leg demurely tucked behind the other. And with one last longing look at the door Claudia eased down onto the gold-striped sofa opposite.

Staff came and went, and there was no mistaking the questions in their eyes as they surreptitiously glanced her way. The need to reach up, touch her face just to check, was so all-consuming, she trembled with the power of it. So she folded her hands atop her lap, so tightly her fingers wept. She could feel Lucas's intense gaze—was he thinking the same as her mother? The same as everyone in this room? That she didn't belong. That she looked out of place.

Suddenly her mother's voice smashed through the thin veneer. 'The ball is Saturday next, Claudine. I shall arrange for a selection of gowns to be delivered.'

Mask rigid, her mind screamed. *You can dress me up like a china doll but lavish fripperies can never veil the woman I am inside.* A woman as far away from being a princess as her mother was from having a heart.

Did she feel anything? Claudia wondered. Had this picture of perfection felt anything the day she'd said Claudia wasn't beautiful any more? The day Claudia's nightmares had been born, and the horror that had finally sentenced her to extradition? Maybe her mother didn't remember the terrible things she'd said, done. But Claudia would. Until the end of time.

'Then, once you are settled and back at the palace,' her mother continued. 'we can discuss the future.'

Slam went her defences as they locked into place and her

head jerked upright. Future? Her future was in London, where she'd built her life: 'I have three weeks' leave, Mother. That is all.'

'Let us not place time restrictions on ourselves. Now you are home it is important we get to know each other once again.'

Once again? She doubted if her mother even remembered her first steps, never mind her favourite book.

'And we have a couple of weeks to do so,' Claudia said, her tone sharp, slicing through the room. She'd fought for years and she was *never* giving up her freedom.

Unfazed, her mother went on. 'Andalina also returns tomorrow, from New York, and Luciana flies in from Singapore the day after. It will be nice for you girls to come together.' Her voice was laced with...*pleasure?* 'Show our country a united front.'

Claudia crushed her lips. Oh, of course. The reason she'd been torn away from her job saving lives and curing pain was to play happy families. Yes, she wanted to see her sisters again, but how could she possibly compare to their scandalous, famed-for-their-beauty presence?

She couldn't. It was impossible. She almost told her mother so. But then that red river of screaming returned to sluice beneath her skin. Because she could hear Lucas making his excuses to her father, declaring his intention to leave. And she knew.

Lucas was leaving her here. Either he didn't want her with him or... Oh, God, had her father insisted she stay here?

'Your Royal Highness?'

And there it was. Her title. Not *Just Claudia.*

Discreetly she inhaled a fortifying breath, perfected serenity and looked up to where Lucas stood beside her, an enigmatic hardness to his gorgeous face. Every delicious atom of his being oozed military man dominance—his duty to king and country was in his every powerful step. Her heart throbbed.

Her mind yelled. *Don't do this, Lucas. Please don't break your word to me. Not you.*

Intense sapphire eyes bored into hers. 'Come. It is time to leave.'

Lucas kept his stride short as they walked across the court-yard to the helipad. Not an easy feat for a man with extra-long legs, but he sensed Claudia was at the very edge of her limits. Even with her damn façade in place. *Dios,* his vision of a heart-warming reunion had just been exploded with a double-barrelled shotgun.

The sound of her feet scoring asphalt, as if she were about to trip in her haste, was a kick to his protective gut and he snagged Claudia's arm, tugging her into a darkened corridor leading to the armoury.

'Breathe, Claudia.' Grasping her shoulders, he manoeuvred her to lean against the stone wall…then backed the hell away. Before he hauled her into his arms. The situation was already complex enough. But, *Dios,* she wanted him to. He knew from the way her eyes devoured his wide shoulders, his chest, even as she wrapped her own delicate hands around her body.

He clenched his fists so hard a spear of pain lanced up his forearms. 'Why are you running?'

'I'm not running anywhere,' she said, still breathless. 'We're leaving…aren't we?'

Lucas thrust his fingers through his hair. '*Sí.* After you calm down, speak to me.'

Closing her eyes, she gently banged her head on the stone wall—once, twice. 'God, Lucas, what do you want from me. I came, didn't I? Just like you wanted.'

'No, just as your parents wanted.' Yet there had been no embrace. No words of joy. Only duty. While he understood duty took priority over all else, pure empathy had torn through him as he'd watched her encounter such insouciance. After all she'd been through.

A humourless laugh slipped from her lips. 'Oh, yes—except they want someone who doesn't exist.'

Lucas frowned. 'Explain this to me.'

'I can't be what they want,' she said, her voice pitching with frustration. 'Do I look like a princess of the realm to you? No. What if I embarrass them in front of the world? Make some pithy remark to the King of Salzerre? Look ridiculous in some frou-frou dress with no sleeves—?'

'Look at me,' he demanded.

When she did not obey he slid his fingers up her jaw, cupped her face and tilted it to look at him. He felt himself almost drowning in her amber eyes. Eyes that were now brimming with hurt.

'No more excuses. You must believe in yourself. In what you are capable of. As I do.'

'You…you do?'

'*Sí.* Of course. Do you know what your people call you, Claudia? The Lost Princesa. How right they are—for still you are lost. When I saw Bailey I knew. You hide. You need to break free. Show them who you truly are inside. The rest will come.'

He could feel her pulse thrumming against the ball of his hand, her throat convulse.

'Being back here—' Her voice cracked on a whisper. 'I'm twelve years old again. So sick. So cold.'

A giant fist punched him in the guts. 'You have bad memories of being here.' It made perfect sense, but there was more, he knew. Problem was, he was treading perilously close to quicksand. For her relationship with her parents, however awkward and frigid, was none of his business. Still, he was unwilling to watch her fall or unveil another damn façade.

'You are sick no more, Claudia. While I am angry as hell that life has dealt you such a card, you have found your way. You have become an accomplished, intelligent woman in your own right. Be proud of this.' With his thumbs he drew small circles on her soft cheeks, luring her in to believe him. Fighting the craving to kiss the sadness from her lips. 'Be proud of your brave heart.'

'I don't feel brave,' she whispered. 'I feel lost. I know my role back home. I know my job. Here—I'm not one of them. I don't know how to be.'

Lucas pulled back, his hands slipping from her face to rake around the back of his neck. 'And do you think I did?' he asked, aggravated by the tightness in his voice, yet determined to show her he understood. 'I was not born to this world, Claudia. Far from it.'

Her lips parted on an indrawn breath. 'But you're perfectly at ease here.'

'*Sì.* I too had to learn. And I found honour in doing so.' He'd found more than honour. He'd found a way of life. One that had saved him from the dark side. Given him the strength to move on, to fight. 'Fear has no place in your heart right now.'

Eyes firing with the first spark of that spirit he craved, she said, 'I'm not scared. I—' Her brow creased as she bit her lip. 'Maybe I am. A little. But you said so yourself. I look *dour*. I can't be elegant like *her*. Like my sisters. It's impossible.'

Lucas raised one brow and gave her The Look. 'And where is the woman who told me only yesterday that nothing is impossible?'

Lips curving sweetly, sadly, she said, 'I have no idea.'

'Then let us find her.'

CHAPTER EIGHT

THE NEXT MORNING, Claudia feast her eyes upon the orange groves lining the driveway leading from Lucas's estate to the open road and nestled closer to the car door, depressing the window button with the tip of her finger.

An intoxicating sweet scent drifted up her nose, filling her lungs until she never wanted to exhale.

'I'd forgotten,' she said, 'The amazing smell of orange blossom.'

It seemed to cling to her senses, stir something deep inside her...something long forgotten. A surreal feeling of peace washed over her—a sensation that didn't make any sense.

'It is heavier during spring when the trees are in full bloom. More decadent, I think.'

Lucas's deep masculine voice overwhelmed her and made her headier still, her pulse skipping.

Tilting her head to peek skyward through the large gap in the blackened window, she closed her eyes, basking in the morning sun, wondering about the kind of man who proclaimed he didn't feel and yet used the word *decadent*. *The same man who is sheltering you from the storm.* But that, she told herself, was Lucas doing his job. Keeping her in Arunthia to fulfil her duty. A role which had once again kept her eyes wide through the night. But when the dawn had come so had her vow. If Lucas believed she could pull it off and play princess for the night she would give it her best shot. If only to prove to herself that she could. That she wasn't shackled by the past.

Heavenly rays stroked through the clusters of fruit, the light speckling over her face. Shadows came and went, during which time she could just make out the tiny white flowers clinging to the bulbous dewy fruit.

'Are they still Arunthia's main export?'

'Yes. Although as a country we are now richer from other timely investments. Mango, grapes, olives—that kind of thing.' Leather creaked as he shifted on the seat beside her. 'You are too hot, Claudia.'

'I know,' she said, tugging at the neckline of her long-sleeved tunic.

'Close the window and the air-con will cool you.'

'I need something cooler to wear.'

Black was no good in this horrid heat. And close proximity to Lucas didn't help. If she hadn't been distinctly uncomfortable in her own skin before she was now.

'I have already made an appointment for you at the boutique in town.'

A moan slipped past her lips. Why, oh, why had she agreed to this? *Come on, Claudia. We're talking clothes, not strains of cholera.*

'Afterwards we will take a stroll. Today is market day, I believe.'

Another moan. 'Don't feel the need to ease me in gently, will you, Lucas? This isn't one of your military operations. At least allow me time to feel comfortable in full regalia before a full inspection.'

'Dream on, Claudia.'

Was he smiling? She didn't dare look in case she melted.

'The people will see you and you will dig deep for that inner radiance and that beautiful smile of yours.'

She blinked. The scenery shuttered in and out of view. That was the second time he'd put her name and the word beautiful into one sentence. Wait a minute... *Inner radiance?* Was he high? Unable to resist looking at him for a second longer, she twisted at the waist and braced herself for the habitual hormone overload. It didn't work. Utter waste of energy.

Absorbing eighty percent of the oxygen and encompassing ninety-five percent of the space, Lucas was a modern-day gladiator. Leaning pensively on his wrist as he took particular interest in the opposite side of the road.

With a quick glance to check that the privacy glass between themselves and Armande was firmly in place, she snapped back to him, 'I think you need your eyes tested, Lucas.'

Fist dropping to his lap, he turned and speared her with his don't-mess-with-me look. 'It is you who needs an eye-test, Claudia. Maybe then you would not wear reading glasses for long distance.'

She gawped. Outright glared at him. 'You're beginning to scare me, do you know that?'

He smiled. The brute actually smiled. And—oh, boy—her stomach flipped, then fluttered as if filled with white blossom bobbing on a breeze. It was a lopsided sinful smile that was loaded with bad-boy charisma. Just a hint of straight pearly teeth and a dimple in one cheek. Licking her lips, she'd swear she could taste that gorgeous mouth of his.

'A shield, in whatever form, only hides so much,' he said, before shifting on his hip and reaching up to where her glasses sat visor-like atop her head. 'You do not need them for visiting, for shopping, for the breathtaking scenery or as a hairband.'

His husky voice… The slide of his fingers, abrasive on her scalp…

'Do not deny people the pleasure of seeing your amber fire.'

Amber fire?

'How do you do it?' she asked, a little breathless, a whole lot stunned. 'You soak in every nuance. It's really intimidating. Am I so easy to read?'

'No. You have many layers and they are proving hard to strip away.'

Strip? She wished to God he'd strip her right now—or take

off his own clothes. She wasn't picky. Against all logic she wanted to touch him. With one kiss he'd given her a taste of undiluted desire and like a potent drug she craved another shot.

Thought vanished as he pulled her glasses free and the light scrape of his fingers brushed across her cheek. She focused on his eyes. Rich dark blue, hot and intense, pupils dilated.

Claudia held onto the moment and the past forty-eight hours disappeared. She could feel him surrounding her—hard and fiercely passionate. The seductive pull of his mouth. What would his mouth feel like on her neck? Her breasts? Her stomach? What would he feel like deep like inside her?

Something hot and sultry splashed through her midsection and she gripped the edge of the buttery leather seat with one hand and squeezed her thighs together. *Oh, God,* what was happening to her?

Lucas broke the connection and closed the arms of her glasses in on themselves. Bereft, Claudia watched him plop the frames into the cubbyhole lining the door, delve into the inside pocket of his suave black jacket and pull out a platinum-encased pen. Lowering his eyes to the small table in front of him, where a sheaf of papers lay, he began to scrawl his signature, his long fingers stroking the silver column.

Visions—vividly sensual and achingly explicit—poured into her mind. Where they came from she had no idea, but she couldn't seem to stop them. Clenching her insides, she wriggled to ease the damp sensation between her legs and pulled at the small window button to douse the sweet bouquet of nature. Only to be ensnared in a whirlwind of musk-drenched pheromones.

Vision blurring, she squeezed her eyes shut. 'How far?'

'Ten minutes,' he said, in a growl she'd come to recognise as Lucas being unhappy with her. 'Nine.'

He was on a countdown. Nine minutes? Heavens above, she'd be a puddle in the footwell by then. She rubbed her brow, felt the moisture coat her fingertips and tore at the high neck of her tunic.

Lucas reached for the control panel between them and lowered the temperature in the car by four degrees. He might as well have hiked it up, because the sight of his long thick fingers stroking the controls detonated the nuclear bomb in the pit of her stomach and she began to literally quake.

'Are you car-sick?' he asked.

Sick? She was sick in the head. This had to stop! Frantic, she dug deep to unearth hate and came up blank. When had that happened? Yesterday, when he'd swept her away from the palace? Or when he'd slanted that hot hard mouth over hers? Or had it been when he'd been so damn wonderful with Bailey?

'Claudia, did you hear me?'

'Sick. Yes. Terribly.'

Okay no hate. What else did she have? Well, for starters, he didn't want her. Wasn't it mortifying enough that one kiss had put him off? And she didn't even know him! While he was stripping her bare—somehow with all her clothes still intact—she still had no idea who he was.

Lucas lowered the privacy glass to speak to Armande. 'I will tell him to pull over.'

Claudia gripped his arm, tugged. 'No. Not that kind of sick. Just…' She flicked her shoulder, scrambling for a word. Any word. 'Nervous. Just nervous. Carry on. Honest.' The more time they spent in this car, the more chance she had of making a fool of herself.

Up went the glass partition, yet his searching eyes never left her face. Since she'd moved to grab him they were too close, but she couldn't seem to let go—just luxuriated in the touch of fine wool and hot steel beneath. Colour scored his cheeks and she watched, mesmerised, as his throat convulsed, a muscle ticked his jaw.

'*Dios,* I cannot continue travelling in these confined spaces with you. It is agony.'

There it was. It shouldn't hurt. But it really, really did.

She snatched her hand away. 'Agony. Right.' While she was

burning up, ready to spontaneously combust, he abhorred their close proximity.

Slamming the table upright with one hand, he shoved the papers in his briefcase with the other. Breath short, his chest began to heave, and his amazing blue eyes speared an arrow of heat straight to her core. '*Dios,* your brain is addled. And I am running out of ideas on how to convince you.'

'Convince me of what?'

'That you were not born to hide!'

'Hide? You're not making sense.' And why was he always so angry with her?

'Tell me, what do you feel like right now? In here?' he said, punching his own rock-hard stomach. 'Truthfully, Claudia,' he growled in warning.

On fire. A tight fusion of energy cells clustered into a fiery ball—sparking, fighting to explode. As if she had the worst stomach ache on earth. Or was it the best stomach ache on earth? Regardless, if she moved one muscle and rubbed down *there,* where her knickers were so wet, she'd seriously...

'Agony,' she said, the word slipping out before she had a chance to stop it.

'*Sí.* Agony. As do I.'

Her eyes slid to where the expensive weave of his suit pulled tight around his thick thighs and groin. He couldn't possibly...

'Oh,' she said a little shakily as her insides grew heavier still.

Tucking one of his fingers under her chin, he raised her head until their eyes met. 'You are clueless, Claudia. You think I could devour you like that and feel nothing?'

'I just thought...maybe you kiss everyone like that.'

His chin dipped as his eyebrows shot skyward. 'I appreciate your confidence in my abilities.'

'And you pulled away. In fact you pushed me away!'

'*Sí,*' he said, ripping his finger from her chin so quickly her head bobbed. 'For my own damn sanity and your honour. Before I took you against the wall.'

'Oh? It was good, then?' she asked, trying to quell the initial elation and excitement until she knew for sure.

Facing front, he thrust his fingers through his hair and clawed down his face. 'And now I finally see what has been staring me in the face. Tell me, when you look in the mirror, what do you see?'

Shaking her head, she inched backwards. But given the space deprivation she didn't make much progress.

'Exactly,' he said, turning back to face her. 'You do not like what you see.'

She tore at her lip. Why was he persecuting her like this? In truth she couldn't remember the last time she'd peered at her reflection—-except for in the en-suite bedroom in Lucas's penthouse. Because she loathed every flaw. Wondered if every slight shade variation on her skin was her imagination or a sign of something to come.

His eyes darkened to the colour of midnight. 'Why? I ask myself. When you are the most beautiful woman I have ever seen.'

Stupefied, she parted her lips as a war erupted inside her— her mind tripping over disbelief, her heart squeezing at his earnest words. Because she knew he wouldn't lie. 'Oh…'

Lucas snorted. 'Suddenly you have lost your internal dictionary. It seems I have found another way to shut you up. I shall remember this.'

'I preferred the other way,' she said, remembering the way he'd backed her up against the car outside her flat. She'd been right! He'd been going to kiss her. She wanted him to. Right. Now.

He laughed without a speck of humour. 'Do not even think about it.'

'Well, why not? If I want to and you want to… Couldn't we just…?' She wanted him to kiss her again so desperately she smothered her lips in moisture. Maybe if he touched her, put his hands on her breasts, they wouldn't ache so much.

'No. *No.* And do not look at me in that way!'

'I'm not,' she said, before his words registered. 'What way?'

'With those slumberous eyes and that sexy mouth. I—' He groaned and flung himself back into the seat.

She had a sexy mouth? 'So where's the problem in that?'

'The problem with that, Claudia, is that along with your beauty I see a woman who I am forbidden to touch—and no,' he said, palm facing her in a stop sign, 'I am *not* only talking about my position at the palace. I am talking about my life. My rules. Did you not listen to a word I said yesterday? I have *sex*. Pure and simple.'

'Really?' It sounded kind of exciting to her. She'd never done anything exciting in her whole life. If just the idea exploded some of those fiery cells inside her, imagine what thrilling ecstasy she would experience if they actually did it. Although she guessed excitement was the improper response, because Lucas had seemingly caught the stimulated pitch in her tone and grim contempt slashed across his face.

'It is just sex, Claudia. Meaningless. A short diversion with women I do not know. Woman who comprehend that I will leave and never, *ever* come back.'

When he said it like that, so cold and detached, she felt a shiver swarm across the base of her spine. He left. But didn't everyone? Of course they did. Except this time *she* would be leaving. After this trip she'd never see him again. She knew that. And surely the hollow pang she felt inside her at that thought was only because Lucas kept distracting her at breakfast.

'*Sí.* Now you understand,' he said, somewhat relieved.

Yes, clearly he used women. But surely they used him too? For pleasure? What was so wrong about that? Now she knew the attraction was reciprocated it was her chance to experiment with her body, explore all these new and fantastic sensations. When his lips touched hers she forgot everything. The past. What was to come. And, in truth, she wanted to experience being desired, wanted. Just once in her life. She'd never trust another man as long as she lived.

'I am hard, unfeeling,' he bit out. 'I am not a man to become attached to. *Comprende?*'

Claudia began to wonder who exactly he was trying to convince here. She nodded. 'I'm not deaf, Lucas, I understand perfectly.'

Good grief, the last thing she wanted was to become *attached* to the man. Apart from the fact he was emotionally void, he lived in a different country. She was going home in three weeks—back to her life, to London, to Bailey. And she might trust him with her life but she'd never trust him with her heart. Claudia knew the price of loving, of needing. Inevitable heartbreak.

'Bueno,' he said, giving her a searching look, not entirely convinced. 'Good.'

'You just have sex. You don't get involved. You walk away,' she said, warming more to the idea with every passing second even as her body was shaking itself apart with adrenaline. No emotions. The thrill of undiscovered excitement. One taste of passion: a memory to last her a lifetime. And, more importantly, *Claudia* would be the one to walk away. 'And you find me b...beautiful, right?'

He blinked, worked his mouth round the word. 'Yes.'

'That's okay, then. Because I just want sex too.'

A stunned light flashed in his intent stare. *'Madre de Dios!'* he said, raising his hands as if praying to the heavens for patience.

'I do.'

'*Si?* Well,' he said, with caustic bite, 'we both know that oftentimes your sense of self-preservation is severely lacking.'

'But I—'

'No, Claudia. No buts. It is impossible.'

The slash of his hand acted like a zipper across her lips.

Slumping back onto the leather seat, she fastened her eyes on the view. Watched the flashing images of small stucco homes as the car sped through the outskirts of town—everything a blur.

Maybe she hadn't handled that so well. Obviously he thought she'd want more than he could give. So she had to convince Lucas that beyond this visit and her obligation to play princess for the night of the ball she was *Just Claudia*. And *Just Claudia* wanted exactly the same thing he did. No commitment. No messy entanglements. Just sex.

The question was: how did she convince him of that?

A blast of trepidation evaporated the moisture on her nape as she remembered who she was—gauche, fidgety and, to use one of Lucas's words, *clueless* in the art of all things sexual.

Her stomach hit the leather with a disheartened thump.

Lucas's women were no doubt the opposite of her in every way—glamorous spelk-like things who knew what they were about. Knew how to lure, to seduce. She wouldn't know where to start. And how could *she* possibly satisfy a veritable god of war and passion? It was the most ridiculous idea she'd ever thought up. So why did it also feel like the most wonderful?

Risking another look at him, she bit her inner cheek.

Fingers curved over his mouth, he stared into the distance, his other hand clenching and releasing where it lay on his thick thigh. One look and that wicked, salacious torrent doused some of her unease. She brushed her hair from her face with the back of her unsteady hand and straightened in her seat.

Fear has no place in your heart right now.

She could do this. Absolutely. He was worth it. She wanted a taste of passion. Just once in her life. And she trusted him. It was perfect.

She could do this.

After all, had he not told her she was capable of anything she put her mind to?

CHAPTER NINE

THAT'S OKAY, THEN. Because I just want sex too.

Lucas scratched his name along the bottom of another LGAS contract, no doubt scoring the wood beneath, then flexed his neck, rolling the stiffness from his shoulders.

Dios, the woman was going to be the death of him. And, although she'd seemed to accept his 'impossible' decree in the car, he could not shake the sense that he was staring down the barrel of a gun.

'I'm done. We can go, if you're ready.'

Claudia's soft voice, a tad apprehensive, drifted from somewhere over his left shoulder.

'*Sí.* One moment.' Feet flat to the floor, he pushed his chair back from the small table where he'd set up a temporary office in the corner of the boutique. Twisting at the waist, he bent double and wedged the papers back into his briefcase on the floor.

The click-click of heels on parquet snagged his attention and his gaze darted to a pair of… He swallowed. A pair of sexy-as-hell black peeptoe heels, adorned with a diamond and sapphire-encrusted brooch just above small toes.

A tsunami thundering through town couldn't have stopped his eyes from doing a slow glissade over sculpted ankles, up over sleek honey-gold skin that sheathed the sexiest pair of calves he'd ever seen…until they disappeared at the knee beneath the flirty edges of a sapphire-blue pleated skirt. No, he amended, his heart thumping in his chest, it was a dress, skimming the lush flare of her hips, cinching the small span of her waist with a black silk sash. At the full curve of her lush breasts his eyes lingered, just a beat, before rising to the slash neck and floating down the length of her arms to stop at her wrists.

His pulse spiked so hard a shaft of pain shot across his chest.

A delicate throat-clearing made him blink. He was half out of his seat, staring like some doe-eyed recruit, for God's sake.

Lucas bolted upright. The chair hit the floor with a thud and his eyes careened into Claudia's.

'Do I look okay?' she asked, head canted, sucking provocatively on her lower lip, her brow creased in an endearingly nervous little frown.

'*Sí*,' he said, searching for the right words, cursing himself that he was ill equipped to do her justice. *You look beautiful* wasn't quite right, because nothing on earth was as beautiful as her face. Sophisticated? Or just downright knee-knockingly gorgeous? In the end he settled for the absolute truth, knowing she needed to hear it. 'Words fail me, Princesa.'

One corner of her delectable mouth lifted. 'That's good, right?'

Shrugging, he made his reply lazy, despite the magnitude of its importance. For it was extraordinary to believe a woman of such beauty disliked her own reflection. Believed she was imperfect in any way. When in reality the only thing she lacked was self-confidence. Well, not today. '*Sí*. Very, *very* good. It is also unheard of.'

Her smile blazed to killer proportions before she gnawed her lip and slowly, warily, closed the distance between them.

'Claudia?' he growled, not liking where this was going. Or possibly liking it too much.

Being assailed with her vanilla-drenched scent doubled the dose of want and he stiffened from top to toe as she curled her fingers round the lapel of his jacket, tugged…rose on her tiptoes and dropped a delicate kiss on his cheek, whispering, 'Thank you…' against the sensitive skin on the underside of his ear.

A shudder racked down his spine and he fisted his hands to stop himself from hauling her close. Instead he watched her long nimble fingers stroke down the lapel of his jacket—an innocent touch he swore he could feel against his bare skin—then turn on her kitten-heels towards the door, hips swaying with a natural hypnotic rhythm that distorted his vision.

'Lucas, are you coming?'

No, unfortunately not. Although if she kept touching him…

What the hell was she thinking, kissing him like that? When he'd already told her no! *Dios,* maybe he was over-analysing what could have been a simple thank-you.

Discarding his unease, he snatched his briefcase from the floor and strode towards her. 'Give your bags to Armande and we'll walk through town.'

The assistants scurried over with an armful of bags, a pair of large sunglasses and a black hat trimmed with the same blue of her dress. Claudia eased the hat atop her head and slowly pushed the glasses up her nose.

'Camouflage, Claudia?' Although he had to admit she looked stunning. Like the front cover spread of some glossy American magazine.

'Baby steps, Lucas.'

He didn't bother telling her she was wasting her time.

As predicted, flying under the radar had become a distant memory, because every pair of eyes swung in Claudia's direction and locked on target as they sauntered down the main avenue—his favourite part of the old town.

Blossom trees lined the road, branches heavy with a full show of colour, and the light breeze wafted tiny pink and cream petals in every direction to settle on the cobbles beneath their feet.

'Now I know what it feels like to be a cell on a slide,' she said, tugging on the sleeves of her dress in that habitual way that drove him *loco,* before inching closer as if needing to absorb his strength.

'Let them see the Lost Princess has returned.'

'Is that why they're staring so much?' she asked, her honeyed voice tainted with amazement. With a discreet jerk of her head she motioned up ahead. 'Even him?'

Pausing mid-stride, Lucas looked up to see a young hotshot sitting on one of the stone benches lining the street, leering at Claudia with blatant lust.

Locking a growl in his chest, he curved his arm around her small waist, protectively, and steered her past, ignoring the slow burn up his arm. It was untenable to realise the ramifications of her illness.

'Has it never occurred to you that after you recovered from your illness people would look at you for an entirely different reason? Men would stare because they were enthralled? Women would stare with envy?'

'N...no,' she said, stunned, and breathless as she sidled closer still. 'Not once.'

Dios, little wonder there had been no men in her life. 'Well, now you know,' he said, dropping his arm as if she were a grenade. Before he nigh on detonated.

'As for the rest—remember you are a mystery to them.'

On cue, a small girl tentatively approached Claudia, all long blonde curls and sweet smiles as she curtsied and bestowed upon her a small posy of lilacs from behind her back.

Claudia blinked as if the child were an apparition, then bent at the waist until they were at eye level. In the same rich-with-affection tone she used with Bailey—the one that made a strange yearning pour through his soul—she said, 'How beautiful you are. I shall treasure them, for they are the first flowers I've ever been given. Thank you.'

A wild torrent of feeling flooded down his chest. How could that be? Had her parents never sent her flowers? Even on her birthday? Claudia turned to him, her forehead nipped, as if trying to suppress the power of her emotions. And a memory slammed into him, making the world tilt on its axis. His mind flickered...

There he was. His ninth birthday. His mother—so soft, so

sad—trying to smile through the pain of a broken jaw. A small box wrapped in her favourite blue headscarf. A car—a toy Ferrari. The brightest shade of red he'd ever seen. His throat closed, his heart bleeding, when he realised the exorbitant price she had paid. *Dios. Breathe, Garcia. Breathe.*

'Lucas?' Claudia's voice, rich with affection, tainted with concern, drifted on the sweet-scented air and he fisted his hands to stop himself reaching out, hauling her to him, burying his face in her neck, breathing her in.

'Are you okay?'

'*Sí,*' he said, slamming the door on the past. 'Do you like your gift?'

She tried for a smile. One that cut him to the core.

'Arunthia holds its royal family close to its heart. And your career has made you very popular with the people.'

'I didn't think…' Her husky voice cracked.

'That you were so important?' he asked incredulously.

With a little shake of her head, she tore at her lower lip. 'That I would matter at all.'

Jaw slack, Lucas floundered at the severe lack of her self-worth. 'Well, you are of high import, Claudia. So let them be awed by you. Enjoy it.'

A small huff burst from her lips. '*Enjoy it?*' she repeated, her mood lifting, firing her back into motion to resume their walk. 'That's a bit of a stretch, Lucas. Two days ago I lived in a lab. And, before you say another word, *you* don't care much for attention either. Every time someone bows in your direction I can hear your molars crack.'

His teeth ached just thinking about it. 'Because it is not appropriate.'

'Seems to me you're a local hero, Lucas,' she said, nudging his arm with her elbow, a small smile playing about her lips. '*Enjoy it.*'

A growl rumbled up his chest. 'They are grateful, and I must allow them to show their respect. I have no desire to revel in success when I was merely doing my job and improving the kingdom.' Even then he'd had his own agenda. No one would suffer in filth and violence as his mother had. Not as long as he lived.

A cluster of tables from a café spilled onto the pathway dead ahead and Claudia slid her arm through his, leaning close until he felt the full crush of her breast against his arm.

Lucas ground his jaw. His breathing grew short. 'Let us go back to the car. Down this side street.' Nice. Quiet. Space.

Except the tall stucco buildings seemed to curve inward and Claudia did *not* let go of his arm. Just curled in tighter. And, impossible as it seemed, the silence rang through his head like a ten-bell siren.

'Lucas—earlier, when you—' Coming to a dead stop, she tilted the brim of her hat as she lifted her gaze to a window display, licked her lips. When he finally tore his eyes from that gorgeous mouth he followed her viewpoint to—

Holy...

'Let us move on,' he said, trying to pull her away before his imagination provided him with a view of Claudia dressed in such a thing. But it was much like tugging on the reins of a stubborn horse.

Pressing the tip of one finger against her pout, she focused her gaze, moved a little nearer to the glass plate. 'Do men like that kind of thing?'

Throat thick, he scratched out, 'No…'

'It's pretty, don't you think?'

'No.' Sexy, yes. Seductive, certainly. Erotic, absolutely. *Pretty?* 'Definitely not.'

'Maybe the white one, then?' she said, pointing to a poster of a woman in a tight ivory basque and stockings.

'I know little of these things, but I imagine that ensemble is more suited to a wedding night,' he ground out, attempting another tug, desperation fuelling his force.

Claudia simply let go. And the loss of heat did strange things to his mind-set.

'Oh. I'll never need one of those, then. I couldn't think of anything worse.'

Lucas blinked, scrolled back through the conversation. 'Worse than a wedding night?'

'Getting married.'

She shuddered. Actually shuddered. Why were they suddenly talking about marriage?

Thuds began to pound at his temples. An army of ants began to crawl across his nape.

'I'm married to my job and I always will be. I don't want commitment. I've fought for my freedom and I'm keeping it.'

Lucas's eyes narrowed. 'Every woman wants to get married, Claudia. Surely every little princess dreams of Prince Charming?'

She laughed—mocking, dry. 'I promise you, I've slept through many a dream and Prince Charming has never taken a leading role yet.' With the tip of one unsteady finger she hooked the bridge of her sunglasses and slid them halfway down her nose. 'Do you want to know who has?' she asked, shooting him a look.

On the brink of being coy, that look morphed into something so catastrophically loaded he felt the bullet ricochet to his groin.

Madre de Dios!

'No, I do not,' he said. 'Dreams are private things.' If she ever found out what he did to her in his dreams she would faint dead away.

First kisses equalled purity, and so long as he had breath left in his body she was remaining as pure as new-fallen snow. Whether she liked it or not. Whether she wanted sex or not. And sex, he realised, was exactly what she had on her mind.

Dios, how could he possibly have sex with Claudia? The suggestion was absurd. There were two types of women in the world: those you could slake your carnal appetites on and come away feeling empty and those you made love to. He'd never made love in his life. He wouldn't know how. And Claudia was one of those women. Claudia who wanted sex!

'I've had enough of going slow and talking nonsense. Come,' he said, placing his hand at the base of her spine and giving her a good push.

What she needed was a damn chastity belt. Lucas had a sneaking suspicion he had initiated her into the realms of passion, and the thought of someone else touching her made his fists clench, ready and armed to physically hurt. And just the notion that he might be capable of unwarranted violence...

'You know, Lucas, it occurred to me earlier I know nothing about your personal life,' she said, breaking through his thoughts with the delicacy of a sledgehammer.

'I do not have one,' he said, stiffening against the black twist in his guts.

'Do your parents live nearby?'

'*Si.* In the graveyard.' Ordering his body not to react—even as sweat trickled down his spine—he kept to the basics. Information anyone would know should she dig for dirt.

Feet faltering, she stroked her palm over her heart while her eyes brimmed with empathy. 'I'm so sorry, Lucas.'

Ignoring the dart of annoyance, he shrugged. 'It is the way it is.'

She smiled ruefully. Knowingly. 'Do you miss them?'

'Ah, Claudia, such a tender soul. I was too young. I do not remember if there was anything to miss.' Years he'd managed to erase must remain in the past. For he knew if the floodgates opened he would surely drown.

Even now, standing here in the town his mother had loved, the town he'd rebuilt, those gates rattled on their hinges and water seeped through the cracks, whispering of hunger so deep his stomach would twist. Walls so thin he could hear every scream, every tear. Blood so thick it clotted his hair.

'Oh, Lucas.'

Something snapped inside him. 'Your sympathy is wasted

on me, Princesa,' he said, with satiric bite. 'Save it for children who deserve it.'

He wanted the fiery spark of her temper—craved it. But the little fool just looked up at him, so damn exquisite, as if she understood. She understood nothing.

For a woman who'd been through so much heartache she was astoundingly naïve. Living in her own little bubble. Which made him beyond resolute to protect her from herself. From him.

She had no idea who he really was, what he was capable of. For he too had walked on the dark side. Yet she wanted him with an incredulous passion that now seemed to ooze from her pores, fashioning her with a warm sensual glow.

Bewitching. Precious.

A warning flare—fierce, deadly accurate—discharged in his mind. Lucas had to keep his distance. No more enclosed spaces. No more touching. No more talking in hushed tones or primed glances that made his body seize with a need so fierce he shook with it.

Ignoring the knife-blade to his chest, he faced facts.

He had to kill her feelings dead.

CHAPTER TEN

CLAUDIA LOUNGED ON heaps of velvet cushions atop her bed and pressed 'send' on her latest e-mail to Bailey. The news that the little girl's father was back from the rigs had been the only moment of bliss in an otherwise wretched three days. Days of awkward lunches with her mother. Days since her gauche attempt at seducing Lucas had failed miserably and he'd plonked a barrier the size of the Great Wall of China between them.

If he walked into a room where she was he walked straight back out again. A seemingly impossible feat in a glasshouse, but he always managed to find some place to go. No doubt his office, which was always locked, or the kitchen, which actually boasted walls.

If he didn't have a two-million-pound painting hanging on one of them she would think he couldn't afford plaster divisions at all. Not for the first time she pondered how he was as rich as Croesus. Unless you were the President of the United States no government official could live like this. If he'd ever speak to her in more than one disgustingly polite syllable she would ask him.

Closing her eyes, she banged her head on the silk cushioned headboard. It wasn't that she missed the man—heavens, no—but at home she worked such long hours and here she was just…plain *bored*. So he didn't want to sleep with her? Fine. His version of agony was obviously in a different league to hers. But did that mean they couldn't talk? God, she missed that. And, truly, what was the harm in taking pleasure from his company while she was here?

Swinging her legs off the bed, she surged to her feet. She was going to find the gorgeous brute, act completely normal and convince him to have dinner with her tonight.

Grabbing one of the boutique bags from the floor, she up-ended the contents atop the bed. And groaned aloud at the final laugh at her expense as something slipped from between layers of frothy tissue paper. A swathe of black satin and lace that she swatted to the floor. *'C'est la vie, negligée.'* Then she lifted a coffee-coloured splash of Lycra from the pile and braced her chest for a panic attack.

Bikini.

The beach. Sand, sun, sea and sensitive skin. Just the thought made her pores prickle and her nails beg to scratch but, honestly, she needed air. She could never remember need-ing air before. Then again, she'd never lived with a prime spec-imen of six-foot-plus virile male before. And maybe, a little voice whispered, he would offer to take her down to the beach.

After donning the frighteningly tiny scrap and a sheer mocha cover-up, avoiding every mirror in the room, she pad-ded down the stairs, heading for his office…when she rocked back on her heels. The door to his off-limits space was swung wide, the dark-wood-lined expanse human-free.

'Lucas?'

Only the sound of metal clanging against wood drifted from deeper inside. Without conscious thought she followed the noise through his office, across the plush ivory carpet towards another door at the far side. Several steps led down to another room and, barefoot, she crept down, coming to a dead stop on the last wooden plinth.

She gasped, eyes wide. So *this* was where he hung out. An-other vast expanse, with one wall lined with aluminium cases, locked and bolted to within an inch of their life. A shiver scut-tled through her as she envisaged their contents, yet it wasn't fear for herself that tore through her—it was fear for Lucas.

Being in the military must have placed him in serious danger over the years, and her throat caught fire just thinking about it. Had he ever been hurt? Her stomach ached at the very thought.

Biting hard on her lip, she let her gaze meander to heavy boxing bags hanging from the ceiling, to state-of-the-art gym equipment, the sight of which made her veins throb in an entirely different way and then turn even thicker, even hotter, as she spotted the man himself. He was working his awesome half-naked body so punishingly her heart cracked in two. Why did he do this to himself?

Claudia counted the powerhouse thrusts of his torso up and down, press-up after press-up. The temperature in the room spiked. Her body dissolved in a long, slow melt. She lost count at the two hundred mark as sweat poured off his honed frame, running in rivulets down his temples, trailing over the indentation of his spine as his muscles flexed and bunched.

Oh, my, he was divine.

Snag went her gaze on his left shoulder, where black ink stroked his flesh with the Arunthian crest.

Her molten core spasmed so hard a moan catapulted up her throat. Palm slapped over her mouth, she backed up the stairs. She shouldn't be in here. He'd expressly told her that his office was off-limits. And being someone who hated to be stared at, who loathed the violation of privacy, she was bang out of order watching him at all.

Claudia hit the hallway and ran down the stairs. Suddenly the cool waters of the ocean had never sounded so good. She wouldn't be gone for long.

Lucas would never know.

What was this? The Bermuda triangle?

Fresh from the shower, and after searching the house for over seven minutes, Lucas hurtled back up the stairs, two steps at a time.

'Claudia!'

Had she finally had enough and ordered Armande to take

her back to the palace? It wouldn't surprise him, and in reality he should be pleased. And he *was,* he told himself. But, dammit, she should have told him she was leaving. Just so he knew she was safe. *That* was the reason for the maelstrom of emotion clattering in his chest. Had to be.

Palm flat, he pushed her bedroom door wide, eyes assaulted by the sight before him. *Dios,* the woman was messy. But surely if all her clothes and feminine junk were strewn over every surface she hadn't left him.

Ignoring the warm flush inside, he turned his back on the chaos and strode down the hall to his office. He would ring Armande and see if his right-royal-pain-in-the-ass had asked him for one of her *favours.* The more distant Lucas became, the more she became pally with his second-in-command. And there came another emotion altogether.

Lucas scrubbed his nape. Five days she'd been living under his roof, and already the hair at his temples had turned grey.

Passing the window by his desk, a light flickered in his brain and he turned, looked out onto the private cove. And the air rushed from his lungs....

Dios, the woman was going to be the death of him.

There she was, flirting with the ocean, sheathed in a long-sleeved filmy top that stopped halfway down her thighs. He raked his gaze over her sleek toned legs. Made-for-sex legs. Long enough for her to wrap them around his waist, hook her ankles behind his back and draw him into her hot, tight, wet heat.

Lust punched his groin, the impact jolting him forward. Bracing his hands against the glass pane, he crunched his abs in an effort to stop the blood rushing from every extremity. It didn't help. Not one iota. Watching her play was not in his remit. Her safety, however, was.

Her feet sloshed through the foamy crush as she danced and skipped along the water's edge, using her toes as tiny shovels and kicking the sand high in the air.

With a shake of his head Lucas smiled. For the first time

since they'd met she appeared carefree. Almost happy. It suited her. Elevated her beauty in a way he'd never thought possible.

She faltered, faced the vast expanse of water looking out to sea—and that tiny action made his fingers ball into fists against the glass.

'Do not even think about it, Claudia,' he said, unclenching one hand and stretching for the keypad that operated the high security doors. His hand froze in mid-air as she took a step back, then another, heading back to shore, fingering the hem of her sheer tunic.

Lucas shuttered his eyes against the view, suddenly filled with the notion that he was becoming a voyeur, but his eyes weren't playing the gentleman and opened regardless.

Her fingers still toyed with the hem, as if uncertain, then began to lift the material up her thighs until he could see the low-cut edge of her bikini as it scooped the cheeks of her heart-shaped bottom.

A growl rumbled up his chest. They were like shorts—far sexier than any skimpy triangle he'd ever seen litter a beach. Demure, yet sensual. Head twisting, she looked left and right, as if checking her privacy, then whipped the top clean off her body and tossed it to the sand behind her.

Swallowing hard, he traced the flare of her hips, the small indentation of her waist. *Back off, Garcia. Turn away.*

One of her arms rose, bent at the elbow and pulled a stick—no…a pencil from the huge bun atop her head. His heart stalled for one, two, three beats as her glorious dark bitter-chocolate locks tumbled down her back in a heavy swathe of curls. Falling, falling until they swished around the base of her spine.

Lucas groaned, pushed off the glass, turned…then snapped his head upright. The sudden question of *why* she was stripping darted through his brain and sent his heart into cardiac arrest. Again.

'No. Do not. I warned you,' he said, reaching for the keypad again to unlock the security alarm on the sliding doors, keeping one eye on her as she tentatively stepped out to sea.

His heart slammed against his ribcage. 'You unthinking, senseless…' He punched in the code, eyes darting back and forth from the panel to her. Back to the panel.

Red.

Dios, what was wrong with him?

He tried once more, wondering if the damn thing had jammed, and calculated the time and distance to run through the house. No contest. One more try.

His fingers flew across the pad.

Red.

'Dammit.'

She was thigh-deep, almost at the ledge, and his hands were goddamn trembling.

Sloppy, Garcia, very sloppy.

He closed his eyes, breathed deep, found the higher plain he often visited in the dead of night. Focused on the pad once more. Punched the code a little slower, more controlled.

Green.

Grabbing the lever handle, he pulled the heavy door wide enough to slide his frame through the gap. Then he gripped the steel rail surrounding the terrace with one hand and launched over the side to drop twelve feet down onto the sand, ignoring the shard of pain slicing through his foot.

Lungs tight, he ran for the shoreline. 'Claudia, do not go any further!'

But the closer he got the more he could see she was nowhere near the sheer drop. Yet.

'Claudia!' He hit the water, feet pounding, the sand sucking at his loafers. 'Damn woman,' he muttered, lifting one foot to yank off his shoe, then the other, and throwing them over his shoulder. 'Claudia!' he repeated, closing the distance.

She spun around, her eyes…*alight?* A huge smile illuminated her face. Curls bobbed, caressing her smooth, honeyed shoulders.

'Lucas, look!' she said. 'Fish.'

Bending forward, she pointed to her feet with both forefingers, ramping her cleavage to a lush slit, and his vision blurred.

'I'm in the sea and I can feel squillions of teeny fish tickling my legs. It's amazing.'

She hopped, breasts bouncing, and desire slammed into him with the force of a tidal wave—which did *not* help his current state of mind

'Fish! *Madre de Dios—fish,* Claudia!' he said, balling his hands before he hauled her into his arms, because the need to touch her was so violent he quaked with it. 'What the hell are you doing all the way out here? I told you the sea was off-limits!'

Eerily slowly she straightened, narrowed her eyes, and folded her arms across her taut stomach—the action bunched those incredible breasts above her bikini top, making them threaten to spill over.

'No, you didn't. You told me—and these were your exact words—"No swimming in the sea, *Cllowtia. Comprende?* There is a ledge beyond which a fierce undercurrent could suck you under." That is what you said.'

His chest heaved, *'Sí.* That is exactly what I said.'

'So I'm paddling.'

'Paddling is also forbidden!'

'Forbidden?' she yelled, arms dropping to her sides, hands fisting for a fight, her tone as angry as her gorgeous face. 'What do want me to do, Lucas? Stay in the house while you ignore me or bark instructions as to where I'm going next. Don't I obey your every command? Well, I've had it. It's driving me crazy!'

Getting turned on even more by her temper was probably a bad sign, he thought. 'Quiet and solitude never bothered you in London!'

She seemed to think about that. 'That was then. And I was working. Really, Lucas, don't you think you're overreacting?'

'No.' Although he had to admit from his office she'd seemed a lot farther away.

'For God's sake, can't you forget about your blasted job for one minute?' she hollered.

'My *job?*'

'You aren't going to deprive the country of an apparent national treasure by letting me paddle! And… Oh!'

She scrunched her nose in that cute way she did sometimes.

Cute? Dios, he was losing the plot. She was senseless and selfish and— Wasn't she?

'Ow!' she said, wincing as she looked down. Lifted her foot.

Before she could blink, he shot forward, grabbed her waist and lifted her clean out of the water. 'What is it?'

Her hands clamped on his shoulders, fingers digging into his flesh, and either he pulled or she jumped, because the next thing he knew her breasts were crushed against his chest and her legs were wrapped tight around his waist, hooking at the small of his back.

Madre de Dios!

'Something was getting a bit too friendly,' she said, a little tremble in her voice.

'*Sí.* I do not blame them,' he muttered, distracted by the feel of the soft skin sheathing her decadent curves. *Bad, bad idea, Garcia.* The only thing missing from his earlier erotic fantasy was his carbon-steel erection sliding inside of her. 'You are killing me, Claudia.'

Cupping her delicious derrière, Lucas took all her weight and her fingers slackened their death grip on his shoulders— trusting him, knowing he wouldn't allow her to fall. Such a small thing, but it made his heart stutter and the need to pull her tighter into his body was a ferocious claw. To hold her, just this once, with her glorious hair falling over his bare forearms, a soft and silky caress.

One of her hands slipped off his shoulder, smoothed down his chest, lay over his breast.

'Your heart feels like it's going to burst through your skin,' she said, her voice awed.

'It might,' he breathed, watching her face heat as she stared at his open collar.

With her free hand she tiptoed her fingers to the base of his throat…stroked up his neck and over his jaw, leaving a blazing trail in her wake. And when she slipped her finger between his lips he couldn't resist licking the blunt tip and lightly sucking on her salty flesh.

Fire ignited her amber gaze and through two layers he could feel her pert nipples rub his chest, the erotic graze making him groan long and low.

'This is insane. I have to put you down.' Before he came in his damn boxers. 'Are you hurt?'

'Agony,' she murmured. 'Can't possibly walk.'

His lips twitched. He knew full well they were not discussing her foot, and he turned back towards the house, heading for shore. Which was torture in itself, because with every step the tip of his erection rubbed her moist core.

Dios…

Claudia wrapped her arms around his shoulders. Hung on tight as if she never wanted to let go. Thrust her fingers into the hair at his nape and nuzzled the skin beneath his ear.

'No,' he growled, a shudder racking his big frame.

So of course she did it again, quick learner that she was, and he could feel her lips curve into a wicked smile.

'You haven't shaved,' she whispered. 'I love the rough scrape against my lips. I want to know what it feels like in other places.'

He groaned as the heat built to inferno proportions. 'No, you do not.'

As if to prove him wrong she ground her pelvis against him and Lucas gritted his teeth…he was going to lose it any damn second.

A tiny moan from deep in the back of her throat goaded him…tearing at his precarious hold. And when the hot sand seared his feet Lucas loosened his grip and allowed her to slide down his body. The friction severed the final thread, and he slanted his mouth over hers and kissed her with the full crush of his pent-up desire.

Finally.

Her lips, soft and pliant, felt like heaven, and the last few days and nights of sexual tension drained from his neck, trickled down his vertebrae to pool with more heat in his groin.

Dios, if he were any harder he'd be dead. But still he hauled her closer, pressing her tight against his body and glorying in the sensation of her lush curves surrendering.

Just one kiss, he told himself, needing to assuage the fear that still clung to his brain. One kiss. No more, he bargained. He traced the line of her mouth to be let in—a quick flick to the corner, a soft slide along her lower lip and she parted instantly.

Blood roared through his head, drowning out all caution, and he drove his hands into the thick fall of her hair, holding her head still as his tongue took hers in a wild dance of pleasure. Slip-slide, intense and erotic. All he could think was more...*more.*

Dios, he could kiss her for hours, days, months... 'Claudia,' he said, taking a breath before he suffocated. 'Push me away.'

She cupped his jaw, her fingertips dangerously close to the underside of his ears, and nipped at his lips. 'Make love to me, Lucas.'

His heart crashed against his ribcage. 'No.' Impossible. He closed his eyes. Touched his forehead to hers. 'You need to keep yourself for...'

'I told you—I'm married to my job, just as you are.'

He knew it. Bone-deep, he knew she was right. She was trying while she was here, but as soon as the green light shone she'd be gone.

'I heard you the first time,' he said, tightening his grip on the small span of her waist to grind against her. The delicious abrasion made them moan in unison—an erotic, mind-blowing sound that rent the air.

'Oh, good. Finally we're on the same page. I want you so much, Lucas.'

'Untouched,' he murmured, forcing himself to pull back, needing distance. To breathe. To think.

'Mmm-hmm. And I want you to touch me. Make love to me.'

A fist of panic hit him in the chest. 'I thought you wanted sex.'

'What's the difference?' she asked, dropping lush, moist kisses along his jaw.

She'd never know what the difference was—not if he could help it. Claudia might not want commitment, but she was not some quick, easy lay. The mere thought made his guts twist, made him suddenly unsure if he was capable of being the man she needed.

Slightly distracted by the pulse pounding in his trousers, and the sight of her toned flat stomach leading to the curve of her femininity, it took a huge amount of effort for him to think. 'You should not be so willing to part with your purity for a man like me.'

Slivers of molten anger lit her eyes. 'What man is that, Lucas? The country's hero? My protector?'

'Claudia, you do not know me.' He might be all of those things to her right now, but if she knew the dark truth of his dangerous past—

'I know enough,' she whispered, fisting his hair, tugging gently, kissing his mouth with the moist crush of her lips. 'There's only one man in the world who I want…who I trust. And that man is you.'

Lucas bowed his head. Trust. She trusted him. And he'd never wanted anything more than to taste her. To show her.

Watching the rapid rise and fall of her chest, he stroked up her midriff, ran his thumb along the underside of her breast and felt her stomach spasm beneath his palm. Desperate to see her every reaction, he gazed into her eyes while he cupped one heavy breast, taking the weight, thumbing the tight nipple poking through the Lycra.

'Oh…' Her dark lashes fluttered.

Her legs gave way and Lucas tightened his hold on her waist. *Dios,* she was so responsive. But what if he hurt her?

'Look me in the eye and tell me you don't want to make love to me,' she said. 'If you can, I'll leave. Tonight.'

Everything inside him rebelled. His voice turned thick, pained. 'You know I cannot say that, *querida.*'

'Exactamente,' she whispered, her gorgeous Arunthian accent heavy. *'Bésame.* Kiss me until we can't breathe. Take the agony away. Please, Lucas.'

She opened her mouth and sank her teeth delicately, deliciously into his bottom lip. And he gave up the fight, uncaring of tomorrow, just knowing he needed her, needed this explosion of passion to take him to the edge of the abyss and throw him over the other side.

CHAPTER ELEVEN

CLAUDIA BASKED IN the taste of his wild desperation as Lucas carried her swiftly through the dusk-drenched house, never leaving her mouth.

When they finally reached his bedroom he slowly ended the kiss and oh-so-languidly let her slide down his body until her feet hit the luxuriously thick wool carpet. As he stepped backwards a cool sweep of air dashed over her body and she shivered, the thought of him changing his mind a deep, dark hollow in her soul.

Risking a look at him, she felt the chill evaporate in an instant when, with a sexy smile, he tugged the shirt from his waistband and tore it from his torso, making her insides dissolve into a potent liquid heat.

She'd seen him earlier, of course, but up close he epitomised a modern-day gladiator. Smooth cast-bronze skin stretched taut over military-honed dominating muscle, and his hard pecs flexed as he unsnapped the button of his trousers.

Her breath was now coming in short pants and she swallowed hard. Told herself to look away while he undressed. But she was desperate to watch him, see him. In all his spectacular glory.

The expensive cut of black cloth parted excruciatingly slowly, as if to tease, and she couldn't help the smile toying about her lips. Lucas loaded with bad-boy charisma gave her a swift sharp thrill that made her want to come out and play.

Reaching behind her, she gripped the bikini catch and then stilled—heart thumping against her ribs—wondering if Lucas would like what he saw. Oh, she hadn't thought of that, and she felt the heat leach from her face. But she *was* in a bikini, and really there wasn't much left to uncover, right? And she'd felt his hardness, tasted his passion on her tongue. Now was not the time to torture herself with visions of his other women. He was Claudia's. For now. She didn't need to hide from him. And the hunger to satisfy him, prove she was worth the effort so he'd never regret making love to her, overwhelmed any lingering doubt.

Claudia unsnapped the clasp, rolled her shoulders and watched the coffee-coloured splash drift to the floor at his feet. After a bracing heartbeat she looked up to his face, saw the fierce need in his sapphire eyes and felt a delicious river of satisfaction pour down her spine.

He slowly peeled the material back from his ripped stomach, shucked his trousers to the floor in one deft move, taking his hipsters with them. So self-assured, so brazen, and—*oh, my*—he had every right to be. Not that she had anything to compare except what she'd seen in art—much, *much* smaller—but, hey, intellect told her they would fit together. They had to or she'd die.

Then he cupped her face in his hands, traced the full curve of her lips, the arcs of her cheeks with his thumbs. 'We go slow. I need to know if I...' His throat convulsed. 'If I hurt you.'

Heart-shatteringly wonderful—that was what he was. She wondered if her inexperience was what bothered him the most. It made her even more determined to relax, to make it good for him. 'You won't.'

Lucas lowered his mouth and kissed her hungrily. She melted into his arms, loving the feel of his fevered skin, touching as much of him as she could and brushing up against his hardness. She squirmed, needing him to hurry, to do something to relieve the clenching knot of tension building in her stomach.

'More,' she said against his mouth.

'Slow,' he murmured back.

She groaned as his lips slid from hers, already missing the wild tangle of his tongue, and sucked at her lower lip, wanting, needing, to taste him again.

'*Dios,* you are incredible,' he said, tracing hot, wet, exciting kisses down her throat. And when he reached the spot, just *there,* where her neck met her shoulder, and grazed her with his teeth, nibbled, her stomach spasmed on a rush of heat.

'Oh, Lucas. I…'

She sank her fingers into his hair, twisted, holding on, pulling him into her tighter.

One of his big warm hands cupped her breast, squeezed gently, thumbed her nipple and that was it—her legs crumpled beneath her.

In one swift move Lucas swept her up and laid her upon the bed. '*Querida,* you are so responsive,' he said, his voice pained. 'The smallest touch sets you ablaze.'

'*Your* touch, Lucas,' she whispered, needing him to understand. Only him. There would only ever be him. 'Could you do something about that?'

He chuckled, crawled over her, and braced his arms above her head. 'I know exactly what you need.'

'I'm so glad,' she said, smiling up at him, drinking him in.

Lowering himself to his elbows, his face inches from hers, he swept the hair away from her brow. 'Your glorious hair against my sheets. *Dios,* you are so beautiful, Claudia.'

Her heart cracked wide open at the pure masculine appreciation slashing across his handsome face and she tugged him down for another of his scorching kisses, exulting in the feeling of being wanted, desired.

She writhed on the sumptuous covers as he trailed his lips down her neck, his hand following the curve of her waist, gripping so possessively she shivered.

That same hand curved around her ribs, scooped her breast and—*oh, my*—the sensation of him taking its weight, lapping at her pebbled nipple, before taking the peak into his hot wet mouth to suck gently made her cry out. The high-pitched sound flooded the room, mingling with his hoarse groan.

When he nipped at her wet nipple, teeth sharp yet gentle, she lost control. 'Oh, yes…' She jerked her hips, wanting, needing him to touch her. *There.* 'More.' But the brute didn't seem to care. He merely redirected his attention to her other breast, laving it, taking her higher still.

She phased in and out, the need in her belly curling tighter, more urgent, until she was tangling her fingers in his hair, raking her nails down his wide muscular shoulders.

Lucas tore his mouth away. 'I need to see you. All of you,' he said, sounding a little more desperate, and she revelled in the sudden infusion of female power as he shuffled down the bed, hooked his fingers in her shorts and eased the material down over her hips.

She gripped the satin covers, fisting the cool material in her hands, raised her legs, one and then the other, to help him, squeezing her eyes shut. Oh, God, what was he thinking?

'Open for me, angel,' he said, voice thick.

Angel? Oh, why did that make her feel special? As if she was the only woman he wanted. Could ever want. She shouldn't think like that, but this was a dream and she never wanted to wake up.

Lucas stroked up her thigh, stilled…

Hauling in some much needed bravery, she opened her eyes, saw the look of unadulterated desire slashing his cheekbones crimson. His hair tumbled over his brow as he looked down at the very heart of her and stroked the soft skin of her inner thigh.

Reflexive, audacious, her legs fell wide.

'You are so perfect. Untouched. I need to taste you,' he said, lowering his head.

Her pulse skittered through her veins. 'Er, Lucas?'

'Quiet, *querida,* let me show you.'

One touch of his tongue against her folds and she vaulted off the bed, quivered… Then he took one long, leisurely lick and a cry tore from her throat, filling the room with her passion. He kept on kissing, sucking gently, until the world was spinning and she grappled for safe ground.

Eyes shut, her body arched. She found his head and pushed him deeper, pulled, unsure whether she wanted him to stop or keep going, because she was careening towards something and— 'Lucas, I…need…'

'Let go for me,' he said, before easing one finger inside her and ghosting his thumb over her clitoris…once, twice.

Tension spiralled in her core, winding tighter and tighter as her insides clenched around his finger.

'Ohhh, my G—' She lost her grip, cried out, gasping for breath, her body quaking as the coil unravelled so fast ecstasy shot though her core and lights exploded behind her eyes.

Delirium, she realised, took a while to recover from, but when she eventually came round she prised her eyes open to find Lucas braced above her, palms flat to the bed, a purely masculine, ego-drenched smile across his gorgeous face.

'Better?'

'Amazing,' she whispered, feeling heat scorch her cheeks.

'I've never seen anything so damn sexy as when you come.'

His voice, coarse and needy, gave her the courage to touch him, just as she'd dreamed of.

She stroked his shoulders, down his arms, smoothing her palms over his chest. 'I adore your big hard body, Lucas. Just looking at you makes my stomach flip.'

He smiled with that heart-stopping rogue charm she loved so much and dipped his head, kissed her. The taste of herself exploded on her tongue as she devoured the essence of their mingled passion, until everything began to blur around the edges and heat began to build up again. As if the last twenty minutes had never happened. She'd never felt so alive. So gloriously alive.

As his tongue flicked hers, her fingers became daring and she reached down to touch him. *There.*

A groan rumbled up his chest, 'Careful, *cariña,* or this will not last. I feel like my head is going to explode. Both of them.'

She laughed—happy, carefree, a sound she didn't recognise.

Emboldened, she curled her hand around his satin and steel shaft, dusted her thumb over the taut velvet tip, over and over, just as he had with her.

'Enough,' he growled, jerking from her grasp.

With her eyes locked on his she brought her thumb to her mouth and licked the moisture, tasting his unique blend of salty virility—just as he had with her.

'Dios,' he said, falling on top of her, plundering her mouth until everything spiralled out of control.

Patience evaporated in the searing heat of their entwined bodies. Skin on skin. Their mouths ravenous. Hands stroking everywhere they could reach.

'Wait—protection,' he breathed, pulling away.

'I'm covered,' she said, tugging him right back. She'd thought of that. She wasn't that naïve.

He threw her a questioning look.

'Women's stuff,' she said, reaching up to smooth the crease from his brow. 'Don't stop. Please. I want to feel you inside me.'

'Ah, Claudia, such passion.' He kissed her softly, cupped her breast, squeezed gently. And the heat surged back—greedy, heady, intense.

Lucas manoeuvred until he was settled snugly in the cradle of her thighs and she could feel him nuzzling against her folds.

'Yes, yes,' she said around his lips, wanting this part of him. Shifting her hips, encouraging. Needy.

He slipped inside her, just an inch, and she felt his big body shudder.

'So hot. So tight. I cannot…'

Skin damp, hair drenched, muscles flexing, he was struggling for control, she realised. But he felt sensational and she wanted more.

She lifted her hips.

He sank a little deeper. 'Claudia, ángel, give me a minute.'

He was loath to hurt her, and she adored him for it, but she'd wanted him for what felt like for ever.

Claudia pulled him up to kiss her, tangled her tongue around his, wrapped her legs around his waist, hooked her ankles and pulled him in. All the way.

The air locked in her lungs as she felt a tiny tear inside her. A red-hot arrow lancing up her core.

Lucas tore his mouth way. 'Claudia?' He held her face in his large hands, kissed her mouth. 'Breathe for me, *cariña*.' He skimmed his fingers lovingly down her cheek, picked up her hand, kissed the spot on her wrist where her pulse thrummed against the flesh.

Pain evanesced and she revelled in the fullness, the rightness.

'You feel amazing,' she whispered, staring into his eyes, nearly drowning in the liquid desire pooling in his sapphire depths. And right then, at that very moment, she knew the truth. She was falling. Falling so very hard.

She smiled, imagined it was close to something sad. So she made it brighter, cupped his jaw, massaged behind his ears, his nape, just the way he liked it. She smoothed her hands across his hips. His glutes were like stone. And thank heavens he melted before her eyes.

'I want it all,' she said. 'Take me.'

Even if it were just this once, she needed it to last her a lifetime.

'You feel like heaven,' he said, pulling out of her just a little and then sinking back inside. So gentle, giving her time to adjust. 'So perfect.'

In out, over and over, until all thought was banished and only pleasure remained. Until they found a glorious rhythm and he upped the pace, faster…faster…harder.

Kissing her possessively, he stroked every inch of her, his hand trailing down her thigh as he shifted slightly to deepen his thrust and grind against her where she needed him most.

The new angle spawned shockwaves of fresh sensations and then she was almost there, tightening, crying out, poised at the edge of paradise, reaching for the heights of bliss.

'Claudia…' His huge body stiffened above her and a keening moan seemed to rip from his throat. The exquisite sight of his face contorting with pleasure, tossed her over the edge until she was falling, falling, shattering, revelling in the sensations shooting through her like white-hot stars.

Face buried in the soft skin of her neck, Lucas bathed in her honeyed scent, luxuriating in the aftermath of pleasure such as he'd never known—sure he'd just tasted ecstasy.

Claudia clasped his head, holding him tight. 'Don't let go,' she whispered.

But he would crush her, he knew. So he gathered her in his arms, rolled onto his back until she was sprawled over his chest, her dark tumble of curls a provocative feast.

His heart turned over, struggled to pump blood round his veins, and he closed his eyes while a torrent of conflicting emotions bombarded him. His head was waging an almighty war. *More. Need more. Get up. Move away.* He'd slept with a few women in his time but, *Dios,* nothing like this. This wild, insatiable, clamouring need—this craving to keep her close and never let go. It scared him half to death.

'Lucas?' she said, lifting her head and resting her chin on the back of her hand as she looked up at him. Her eyes were fired with enough anxiety to make his guts clench. 'Was I…okay?'

He let go of the air locked in his chest and raked damp hair back from his brow. Never had he been asked that. But she was looking up at him, so damn trusting, her heart etched on her face, needing to know she'd been worth it. His stomach ached.

'Listen to me, *querida,*' he said, trailing the back of his finger over her temple, down her nose. 'When you are stripped bare and no longer able to hide you are breathtaking.'

As her bruised lips parted he traced them, following the sexy dip of her top lip. Her pink tongue snaked out and flicked the tip and a fresh spurt of heat shot down his spine, thick as lava, as he remembered the way she'd tasted him. Such a ferocious mind. Always learning, always desirous to be the best.

'You're the most passionate woman I have ever met.'

She blinked. Smiled the sexiest of satisfied smiles and dropped a lush, moist kiss on his chest.

'That's good,' she said, as she tiptoed her fingers down his abdomen, cruising over the ridges and down, down to where he was hard and ready for her touch.

Bolder now, she wrapped her fingers around his length and explored every inch of him, first with her hand and then with her eyes. Until the heat was a fiery ball and he was plunging past the point of no return. He grasped her wrist, flipped her over and pinned her to the bed, his hands holding hers above her head.

Her eyes blazed, glittering with shards of exquisite excitement.

'Ah… You like that?'

What she liked, he realised, was to be wanted. She loved his weight on top of her. His strength turned her on, heated her blood. She felt protected. *He* made her feel safe. *Dios.* His heart turned over again. He should not revel in that—he really shouldn't.

Licking her lips, she nodded, her breath quickening, her hips writhing in their own little way to drive him crazy with the need to be inside her.

Keeping her hands above her head with one hand, he trailed the other down the slope of her full lush breast. '*Dios.* You have the body of a goddess. Heavenly to look at. Sinful to touch. Makes me feel damn weak.'

He kissed the soft underside while his fingers trailed down her soft stomach, wanting to see if she was ready. 'You are not sore?'

'No,' she breathed. 'Need you.'

Her head tossed back and forth. Her dark curls fanned over his white pillow. His pillow. His bed. *His.*

Skating over the damp curls at the apex of her thighs, he dipped into her heat, felt warm moisture coat his fingers. A moan—his, hers, entwined—filled the air.

His heart struck up a ferocious beat. Blood roared through his head. Lucas knew he was flirting with disaster, stumbling across unknown territory, yet nothing could stop him. She would be gone soon enough.

'So wet, *cariña*. You want me inside you?'

'Yes, yes…'

Sweat beaded his brow as he settled between her legs, hard and achingly heavy. And when she moved against him for a frantic beat he wondered if he would last.

He grasped her hair, cupped her head in one hand and brought her mouth to his so he could plunder, drink in her cries when she came for him. With his free hand he caught her nipple with his thumb and forefinger, rolling the tight tip until she undulated against him, working up to a frenzy. Then he stroked down her toned thigh and sank into her with one deep thrust.

A hoarse cry broke from his very soul and poured into her mouth. Tight, hot, she gripped him in her slick heat, drawing him deeper under her spell until he didn't know where he ended and she began.

The need to watch her orgasm for him, so he could remember, became an almighty obsession. So he stroked down her waist, over her hip, round to the soft curve of her luscious rear and lifted her thigh-high over his waist to deepen his thrust and grind against her.

'Oh, Lucas…'

Her fingernails bit into the skin on his shoulders and a fever unlike any other took hold of his blood as a torrent of fire built inside him, far stronger than the first time, and Lucas knew—just knew—he would never recover from this explosion of feeling. Never in a million years.

Lips locked, she cried into his mouth, the sound of her sensual elation throwing him over the edge, tossing him into the black depths of ecstasy.

Hurling him into the unknown.

* * *

Light flickered in his brain and Lucas prised his eyes open to the darkness of night. He'd slept?

Warmth smothered the right side of his body and half of his chest…Claudia. She mumbled something, almost a cry, the high pitch snapping him to full lucidity, and Lucas tightened his hold on her waist.

'Claudia?'

She struggled against him and he instantly loosened his grip, cupped the back of her head, softly kissed her temple. 'Wake for me, angel.'

She stilled before the tension drained from her spine and she fell back against his chest. 'I'm sorry,' she said. 'I'm okay. Truly.'

'You were dreaming?'

'It's being back here. So strange.'

Her skin was damp, clammy. 'Not a good dream,' he said. Statement. Fact. Lucas knew too well the cold sweats, the shaking so hard it was impossible even to drink water.

'Not really,' she mumbled, snuggling into his side, hiding her face. 'It's nothing.'

His stomach tensed and he nudged her softly with his arm, needing to see her face. She turned her head and lay down, facing him. 'Do not hide from me, Claudia. I cannot bear it.'

Nibbling on her bottom lip, she gave him a searching look. 'I just have this nightmare sometimes. It's a memory, that's all.'

'Ah, that's all?' he said, trying to tamp down on the flare of anxiety because he knew the power of memories. How they could haunt you. Drain your very soul.

She had demons of her own; he'd known that, hadn't he? 'You tried to tell me on the plane, I remember.'

'Did I?'

That she couldn't recollect spoke volumes. But then he remembered her panic, the fear that had sliced through the very heart of him.

'Tell me your dream,' he said, sweeping a lock of damp hair from her cheek with his fingertip.

He could see the hesitation in her eyes, couldn't understand it. 'Claudia?'

Searching his eyes for a long moment, she seemed to look for sincerity or wonder if she could trust him—not with her body or her safety but with her secrets. Her past.

'Trust me, *cariña.*'

Wriggling from his hold, she rolled onto her back and pulled the sheet up to her neck. Lucas ignored the cold chill sweeping over his body; she needed space. He understood. So he moved onto his side to face her, bent his elbow and rested his head on the ball of his hand.

Staring up at the ceiling, she began to talk, her voice detached. 'I must've been twelve. It's my last memory of being here.' Her brow creased as she delved into the past. 'It was one of those hot clammy days that made me feel so sick I could hardly breathe…hardly walk. My mother took me to the hospital. I think they'd had some specialist flown in.' She shuddered, gripped the sheet at the delicate dip in her throat. 'I could hear every word through the open door, but my legs… I couldn't move to close it. I covered my ears but she was ranting at him. Railing. Going on and on. I'd never heard her in such an awful state.'

She huffed a laugh, the sound so damn hollow his guts twisted.

'You've met her, Lucas. So chillingly calm. So strong. But this day she was almost wild. *"Look at her!"* she screamed to the doctor, jabbing her finger in my direction. *"Just look at her. My beautiful daughter is no more. You have to do something."* On and on she went, for what felt like hours.'

Lucas watched her knuckles scream in protest as she twisted the sheet in her fingers, her eyes closed, her teeth sinking into her lower lip as she stifled her sorrow. And he'd swear his chest had cracked open.

'Someone carried me out to the car. She was so deathly silent and I was so numb. She couldn't bear to look at me. When we reached the Arunthe tunnel there was traffic everywhere.'

Her chest rose and fell with short, sharp breaths and the need to touch her, hold her, was so strong his arms ached.

'I think we'd been followed,' she continued, brushing hair from her damp brow with trembling fingers. 'There was always stuff in the papers, wondering what was wrong with me. Why I was kept under lock and key while my sisters enjoyed their independence. I think being so secretive must've made it worse.'

The room was dim, but Lucas saw one silvery droplet trickle down the side of her face. The pain in his chest tore up his throat. *'Querida—'*

'Suddenly,' she said, 'men were crawling over the car like locusts, banging on the windows so hard I thought the glass would shatter. They yanked at the door handles, over and over, trying to get in. And my mother… She pushed me down—said I had to hide, to stay out of view in case they saw me. *"No pictures of her,"* she was screaming. *"No photos. No photos."* Yelling. Crying. *"They can't see her like this."* I just wanted to die. That's exactly what I wished for.'

Her voice trailed to a pained whisper and Lucas strained to hear her.

'She screamed at the driver to move forward and he tried to switch lanes. He tried. He *tried*.'

Lucas ground his jaw so hard a shard of pain shot up to his temples. 'The car crashed?'

'Yes,' she said, her chest rising as she struggled to wrestle her emotions into submission. 'Next thing I knew I was in London. Hidden. Locked up.'

Her voice ebbed once more and Lucas leaned closer.

'The Princess in the Iron Mask.'

'What?' he said, frowning deeply, sure he mustn't have heard her correctly.

'That's what the other children called me. Although it was probably my own fault. I had at least two copies—you know, the novel by Alexandre Dumas? The mask they needed to hide the face of the King's twin?'

He jerked upright, shaking his head. Adamant. Goddamn furious. 'No, Claudia. *No.*'

'Yes.'

'That was just children being mean and spiteful because you are royalty. Most children dream of such a thing, *querida.*'

She dashed her hands across her cheeks. 'And my mother saying those things? Was *she* just being mean? Telling everyone I wasn't beautiful any more? That she couldn't bear to look at me? Touch me?' Her voice hitched on the last word and she flung back the covers and vaulted off the bed. 'I need to go now.'

'No!' he said, lunging, grabbing her hand, keeping her at the side of the bed until he stood before her. Cupping her face, he looked deep into her eyes. 'Listen to me, Claudia. I'd say your mother was past herself with worry because no doctor could diagnose or even help. She had to watch you suffer. Can you imagine that?' Lucas tilted her face, needing her to see the conviction in his. 'Think of how you feel when you sit with Bailey. It hurts you, *sí?*'

She nodded, just once, eyes flooding, spilling. His heart tore.

'I'd say your mother didn't think or realise the words she spoke would affect you so. Whilst she is not the most affectionate of people, I believe in this case she was unthinking. Not uncaring.'

'You think she honestly cared about me? She cast me out. I was dispensable to them.'

'Impossible,' he said fiercely. 'You are far from dispensable, *cariña.* And you were *not* cast out. The accident, I think, was the last bullet for her. If I had been in the same position and you had almost died I also would've taken you away. Far, far away. Somewhere safe. Where you could get help. St Andrew's is the best—world renowned.'

'And would you have left me there, Lucas? Alone? They hardly came. I waited. And waited.'

His stomach wrenched. Little wonder leaving Bailey had killed her.

Would he have left her? The answer hovered on his tongue. For what peace would it bring her? He could never say the words pounding at his temples, fighting to break free.

'Your parents had a country to run, Claudia—a country in trouble at the time. I remember those years. Your parents had other children. Duty. Responsibilities.' Even as he said the words they sounded hollow, knowing the price she'd paid. Her parents had sacrificed her happiness for the good of thousands. Something he'd done over and over in his career.

'Trust *you* to see it that way,' she said, bitterness lacing her voice, twisting her head until his hands fell away—hands that now felt bereft. 'Of course you'd have left me. Duty. Obligation. That's all you ever talk about. You're just the same as them.'

He closed his mind to the disgust in her eyes. 'I see both ways. For a young sick girl to be left in a foreign country. Isolated in such a way.' His chest felt crushed by the impact. 'It must've been very hard for you.'

He knew all too well the emptiness, the fear she would have felt—could feel it now, brewing in his system like poison. Fear that made you weak. Angry. Resentful. Determined at any cost to close the door to your heart and never reopen it.

'Dios.' The truth slammed into him, almost knocking him off his feet. 'So blind,' he said, scouring her face, drinking in her amazing beauty and tender vulnerability while the last remaining fragments fell into place. The final piece of intelligence he needed to create Claudia Verbault.

'What happened when they came to see you, *cariña?*'

Her gaze fell, drifted to the window as the first strokes of dawn broke through the slit in the drapes. 'I wouldn't speak to them. Not one word. When I grew older, got better, *had* to speak, they started making demands for me to return. I pushed for my independence. I wanted my freedom.'

'No, Claudia,' he said, shaking his head slowly. 'You pushed them away because you were hurting. Your freedom was a ticket to a pain-free zone.'

Her teeth sank into her bottom lip and she finally looked up at him, her amber eyes huge, swimming with unwanted tears. 'Yes,' she whispered, broken, still hurting.

'You believed they would leave you alone. To live your own life.'

She sniffed. 'Hoped would be more like it.'

'Ah, Claudia, all the hope in the world cannot change who you are.' He knew that better than anyone.

No matter the man he'd become, underneath he was still Lucas Allesandro Gallardo—the boy who'd failed to protect and had lost everything. The man who'd fought for king and country and pledged an oath to honour and obey. The same man who'd just surrendered to his selfish desires and taken an innocent. One he'd sworn to protect. A woman he was beginning to doubt knew what she wanted from life, let alone how to find the love she so desperately needed.

She was blossoming before his very eyes—a butterfly emerging from the chrysalis. She deserved happiness and there was a man out there, perfect and strong and made just for her. And now Lucas had ruined her reputation. Lucas who had nothing to offer.

His chest seized, the pain dominant, punishing. She was so damn vulnerable she hadn't realised the consequences of her actions. That had been *his* job. And he'd failed. He'd allowed his emotions to reign. Again. He'd failed to protect. Again.

Lucas closed his eyes. What the hell had he done?

CHAPTER TWELVE

PADDING DOWN THE hallway, Claudia cinched her robe tight. Silence, even after years of it, made her cold from the inside out. What had happened she'd no idea, but after a night of heart-shattering euphoria Lucas was gone. *Her* Lucas, that is.

Lucas Garcia, Head of Security for Arunthia, was back in full military mode today. Distant. Guarded. Re-armed with enough strength to fight a seven-nation army. Even Armande had backed off, when Lucas had gone on a full-on attack over some keypad in his office. But she'd hazard a guess that had more to do with a delivery from the palace—a rack of dresses for the ball tomorrow night and an official-looking parcel for him. 'Business,' he'd said. One of the few words he'd spoken all day.

Feet bare, the chill of each wooden plinth penetrated her feet as she tiptoed down the staircase. Did Lucas blame her for hardening her heart to her parents? It was the hardest thing she'd ever done, and here she was doing it once more.

Thankfully she had more sense than to fall for a man who could make love to her with such glorious passion, then wrap her in one of his dark grey sheets and carry her to her room. Oh, and the real *pièce de résistance* had been the words, 'Go to sleep.' Before the door clicked shut with deafening finality.

He'd walked away—just as he'd warned her he would. So she'd no right to be hurting—*none*.

But…

Sleep? Wrapped in satin that smelt of sex and Lucas?

And still she could smell him—the musky potency that oozed from his every pore. Raw, addictive and utterly tormenting.

A moan snuck past her lips. She just wished she'd never told him the things she had. She might as well have ripped her heart from her chest, sliced it open with a scalpel and laid it on the table for his inspection. Obviously he hadn't much liked what he'd seen.

Pausing on the bottom step, she peered through the darkness, eyes slowly adjusting at the wide rack standing by the window, weighted with a colourful array of cloth. With sleep a pipedream tonight, she'd nothing better to do than make her choice.

Risking a glance at Lucas's office, she saw a thin sliver of light under the door; imagined him sitting there. Honestly, he was such a cold brute at times. Yet it was that very darkness that engaged her—locked her on target and drew her in.

The ivory moon hung low, casting the room in silver swathes—just enough light for her to take a peek at the dresses. When they'd arrived today her bruised heart had demanded they be returned. She could buy her own dress—one that wouldn't come with any stipulations. But then, thankfully, the red haze had cleared and the fact she'd been thought of at all was something. Despite everything they were her parents. And her mother *was* trying.

Trailing her fingers over the array of satin, silk and lace, she closed her eyes. Pale gold ruched satin whispered to her, called her name. Gripping the arch of the clothes hanger, she pulled it from the rack, held it up to her body and swayed gently, watching the frothy skirt swish around her legs. So beautiful. Created for a princess of the realm.

Ramming the dress back on the rail, she picked another. A vibrant aquamarine colour with a low dip at the back, a straight skirt. Full sleeves.

'Ah, Claudia, have I taught you nothing?'

The heavy weight rustled to the floor as she spun around and slapped her hand over her cantering heart.

Lucas lay sprawled on one huge aubergine sofa, where he had a prime-time view of every move she made. One arm bent, he propped up his head, wearing an expression that bordered on dark torment. Hair damp, the dark locks clung to his brow. The lack of light shadowed his blue eyes, transforming them to obsidian depths that drilled straight through her.

His other arm dangled off the edge of the seat, his hand a claw, holding a whisky glass from his fingertips. The crystal tumbler swayed back and forth lazily. Legs wide, one bent knee was resting on the back cushion, the other was long and straight in front of him.

To anyone else it was the insolent pose of a devil-may-care, but Claudia could feel the anguish rolling off him in waves. This devil *did* care, and something powerful held him in thrall.

She feasted on his bronze chest, the rippled curve of his abs and the tight waistband of his black hipsters…and lower to the snug, thick ridge of his erection. A shiver that had nothing to do with the room's temperature whistled through her.

Eyes fluttering shut, she bit hard on her lip, trying to remember why she was so angry with him, shovelling deep to dredge up hurt. She'd been dumped into her cold bed as if nothing had happened between them, then ignored, all day, and lest she forget he'd taken her parents' side over hers. But in all fairness she'd known he would. He was all about duty— just as they were. It shouldn't hurt. It *should* make her heart stronger. Harder.

Counting to three, she ordered her eyes to stay above his waistline and popped them open.

'You've taught me plenty, Lucas. How to reach the heights of passion only to fall from grace. And I have to tell you it's quite a drop. How easy it is to trust, open yourself wide, only to be rejected when you come up wanting. Have my confessions turned you cold? Because, honestly, it's freezing in here.'

'No.'

That was it? *No.* Did she believe him? He certainly didn't have any reason to lie.

Arm lifting, he took another lazy swig of Scotch, his shadowed face haunted, and a pang resounded through her heart.

'Talk to me, Lucas. Tell me what's wrong.'

'Go to bed.' His tone was icy cold, the dismissal cruel.

Curling her fingers into protective fists, she forced her heels into the rug, while the overwhelming urge to go to him, brush the hair from his eyes and kiss away the pain, warred with the fear of rejection. If she could hold him, help him, he might fall asleep in her arms like the first time. How many times had she needed comfort and it had never been offered? Then maybe— just maybe—he would tell her, he would share.

Pushing her pride deep down, knowing he needed her, desperate to console him, she implored, 'Will you come? Spend my last night with me?'

'No.'

One word, loaded with pain.

She took a fortifying gulp of air. 'I don't understand why you're being like this.'

The sound of glass clattering off oak, the slosh of liquid spilling, made her flinch. Not that Lucas seemed to notice.

'Do you realise what I've done, Claudia?' he said. 'Taken an innocent when you were in my protection. I should never have touched you.'

Wait a minute...

'No—*no!* For heaven's sake, I asked *you.* I wanted to make love just once in my life. You've taken nothing from me, Lucas. I gave it freely.'

'Pleasure does not come without a price, *querida,*' he countered fiercely. Then his lips twisted, one dark brow raised into a cynical arch. 'Make love, Claudia? Didn't I tell you I just have sex.'

The way he said *sex,* as if it was dirty, something to be ashamed of, scored at her heart, sent flames of dismay up her throat. He regretted making love to her—having sex—whatever the hell he wanted to call it, and—*oh, my God*—she had to stiffen to stay upright through the pain in her stomach, which twisted tighter with every second he stared, as if he couldn't bear the sight of her. One look that launched a thousand reasons to run. Leaving behind the main reason to stay. Ripping her clean in half.

He was in agony.

Lucas thrust his hands through his hair and tore his eyes from her while a dark torrent stormed through him, pulling, dragging him under. His chest heaved as he suffocated under the dense blanket of remorse.

Dios, he'd taken away her chance of marrying with honour. And that damn letter from her father, pouring out his gratitude to Lucas, had poured gasoline on the flames of his anger. In one night he'd dishonoured her and himself. *Dios,* if their affair ever became public knowledge…

Self-loathing sucked his throat dry.

His gaze landed on the original painting for the tenth time. The memories like a drum-beat, loud and disturbing, warning him to back away, turn her against him, make her leave.

'Who is she, Lucas? You know her. I can see it in your face when you look at her.'

'I do not know her,' he said, his throat thick as he stared at the past. Failure. His mistake. One he would never repeat. 'She reminds me of someone. That is all.'

'Someone you lost?'

He tried to swallow around the grenade lodged in his throat but it was damn impossible. 'Go to bed, Claudia.'

'Talk to me, Lucas,' she begged, taking a step towards him. 'Please.'

Fire and fury bubbled up inside him—a volcano erupting. 'Go to bed,' he repeated louder, far harder than she deserved, which made him feel even more of a bastard.

But, *Madre de Dios,* he was unsure how much more he

could take. Standing before him, she was so damn exquisite. Her eyes full of undeserved empathy.

'Why are you pushing me away?'

His tenuous hold snapped. 'Because I do not want you here. *Comprende?*'

As long as he lived Lucas would never forget the look on her face and his guts twisted, punishing. How could he say that to her? When she already questioned her self-worth? When it was he who was unworthy? And the pain—*Dios,* he hated seeing pain in her eyes. Pain *he* had put there.

Thuds hit his temples. He lifted his hands to cover his burning eyes, but not before a swish of satin whispered by. Like a drug addict grabbing for his next fix, he closed his eyes in ecstasy even as he hated himself for giving in to the hungering clawing need—he grabbed her wrist, pulled, needing to feel her against him and despising himself for his desperation.

Struggling, she pulled her arm away. 'Get off me.'

'Come to me.' *Dios,* the craving was so intense he shook with the power of it.

One quick tug and she was bent over him, her face hovering above his, the soft tumble of her hair brushing his chest and arms, the sweet honeyed scent of purity assailing his mind.

He captured a curl around his finger, mesmerised.

'Let me go,' she whispered, her chest rising and falling, her robe loose, gaping, taunting, teasing him with the lush swell of her breasts cupped in black lace.

Pounding sensations and emotions assaulted him. Relief she was close. Disgust at himself for being unable to let her go. Regret—yes, regret because she didn't deserve to be treated this way. And the ferocious need to replace the pain in her eyes with pleasure. *Will you come? Spend my last night with me?* The pleasure she'd obviously come for.

'Come to me, Claudia,' he said, gliding his free hand up her throat, across the warm skin of her shoulder. Sliding his fingers beneath the satin robe he pushed it down her arm. His sex throbbed for the tightness of her body, but first he needed to banish the anguish from her eyes. 'Let me hold you, *querida*.'

The fight left her then, her glorious body softening. His hand fell away as she stood tall and he watched, bewitched, as the black robe fell from her shoulders in a sensual glide to pool on the floor. It was a damn good job he was lying on his back or he'd be on his knees.

Scantily clad in low-cut lace and sheer black satin, slinking over her curves, she was his every fantasy come to life.

Blood roared through his head as the heat surging through his taut frame built to inferno proportions. 'You're incredible,' he said, grasping her satin-sheathed waist and lifting her over him.

Straightening his legs, he coasted the slippery sheath up her bare thighs so she could straddle him, revelling in the slick skin smothering his hips. He plunged his hands into the thick fall of her hair and pulled her mouth down to his. Kissed her hard, desperate to taste, remember.

He traced the seam of her lips with his tongue. 'Forgive me, *cariña*. It is myself I am angry with.'

'Let it go, Lucas,' she whispered, before her lips surrendered.

The sweet taste of forgiveness coated his tongue and for one blissful moment he allowed himself to savour, to indulge in the forbidden tang.

This was what she wanted, he told himself, what she'd come for. And he'd make it spectacular for her. Make her shatter over and over, make her beg him for more until that fierce brain could no longer think. Only feel. Him. Inside her. Surrounding her. A night she would never forget.

Tomorrow everything would come right. He'd meet with Henri and do what was necessary. And Claudia would stand in front of the nation and accept who she was. She would realise the extent of her duty and responsibilities; his promise to return Princess Claudine Verbault would be complete.

But for tonight she was still his.

Tonight she was still *Just Claudia*.

Her hot naked core nestled against his throbbing erection and she undulated against him with rhythmic serpentine movements that detonated a need that made his vision swim.

'Careful, *cariña*...' he growled.

She filled his mouth with her sweet moans of pleasure. Her hands were a firebrand smoothing over his chest, up the column of his throat, sinking into his hair, massaging the ultra-sensitive skin beneath his ears. It was a confident touch that hummed through his body, and his hips jerked so hard he almost lost it.

In one deft move he broke their lip-lock, whipped the gown up and over her body, tossed it to the floor.

Her voice low and sultry, she began to tell him what she wanted—how hard, how deep, how much she wanted him. Only him. Words he knew were driven by her fierce need for fulfilment and yet he snatched at them, held them close, allowed himself to believe they were true just for a while.

'Lucas, *please.*'

Hand rough, unsteady, Lucas cupped the full swell of one breast, pushed his hipsters down his thighs with the other. She was there, poised, glorious above him. And when she sank down on his erection, sheathing him in hot tight ecstasy, a shot of nitrous injected his heart, stopped it dead.

Claudia's amber eyes locked on his as she flashed him one of her melt-your-knees smiles and flung her head back in wild abandon, arching sinuously. And suddenly that same heart was torn wide open.

He was the mightiest warrior. And he'd just been slayed.

CHAPTER THIRTEEN

A WARM SPLASH of crimson dawn flooded the room, washing his torso in a reddened hue, and Lucas flung back the covers of their makeshift bed, extricated himself from the heady scent of passion and launched to his feet.

Skin damp, flushed, feverish, his body shook as if under the power of some deadly virus. Breathing hard, he thrust his legs into a pair of creased trousers and tied the cotton bands at his waist. Only then did he glance down at Claudia, where she lay curled around his empty space, dozing, cashmere blankets draped over her sinful curves.

Something had gone wrong. Some time during the night. Hours of sex should have at least made him feel sated, at some kind of peace. He scrubbed his palm over the ridges of his abdomen, trying to ease the crush.

Lungs tight, his eyes bounced around the room. *Dios,* he could still see her spread across the glossy black top of his baby grand, open, needy. Still taste the exotic hint of mango on his tongue from when he'd devoured her body. Still feel her nails tearing at his skin.

'Lucas?'

Her voice—small, hesitant—snagged his attention and his gaze jerked back to the mound of pillows. To her.

Dios, the way she was looking at him…

'Come lie with me?' she asked, eyes brimming with hope and something soft and warm.

He shook his head slowly. 'I need to shower, dress.' *Walk away.*

'Okay, well…' She bit down on her bruised bottom lip. 'I've been thinking.'

'*Dios,* Claudia, I wish you wouldn't,' he said, scouring his nape with his palm.

She smiled. 'Ha-ha. Seriously, though, when I go back to London maybe you…'

Lucas closed his eyes as blood began to rush through his skull at a deafening speed.

He'd made a mistake. A colossal error of judgement—something that seemed to be happening with astounding regularity since this woman—*Dios,* no, this *reluctant royal*—had crashed into his life.

Last night she hadn't come to him just for sex, and once again he'd surrendered to his selfish desires. Now she was sussing him out with all the delicacy of a sledgehammer. And never mind London—she needed to take her place at court!

He hadn't heard a word she'd said, but he didn't need to. Her lips had stopped moving and she peered up through long sooty lashes. Coy, sanguine.

Dios, was she falling for him?

Lucas thrust his hands through his hair. Felt moisture coat his palms. 'Claudia, you must see this for what it is. Heat. Passion. That is all there could ever be. We made a pact, you and I.' He had nothing to offer but a dark soul. And he lived only to work—as he should. She deserved so much more—a chance to find the love she needed.

'I know that,' she said, brow creased, her gaze fastened on her nail as she scratched an invisible mark from the throw. 'I just thought if you were ever in London we could have dinner or something. I mean…why not?'

Good question. The answer, he knew, was the cure for the deadly tangle of emotions knotting his guts. Because if she left his life normality, a pleasing lack of feeling, would surely resume.

The only way out was to tell her the truth. Crush any spark, any kindling of emotion that was flickering to life inside of her.

Something made her move. Maybe it was the way his frame stiffened. Maybe his conviction scored his face or maybe she felt the sudden chill nip her skin. Because she bolted upright and tugged a fawn cashmere blanket up over her breasts, veiling herself. Protecting all her heaven while he took her on a trip to hell.

His blood turned black and weaved a poisonous path towards what was to come—the disappointment in her eyes, the mortification—when she realised what kind of man she'd given her body to.

'You asked me last night who she reminded me of,' he said, jerking his chin towards the famous painting. 'The real question is *what* she reminds me of. Tell me, what do you see?'

Her wide eyes flicked to the painting, back to him. 'Pain. She's in pain and she's shielding something. And when you look at her I can feel *your* pain.'

Not for much longer.

'They bear little resemblance, but I knew when I saw her she had to be mine. To remind me of the man I truly am. That I am responsible for her death.'

Drawing her knees up to her chest, she yanked the blanket up to her throat. Her white knuckles stood out starkly against her honey-gold skin.

'While you spend your every waking moment fighting to cure pain, I have *caused* it.'

He watched the flames of her amber fire snuff out. Felt the atmosphere crackle, scratch at his skin.

Fists clenched, he nodded slowly. '*Sí,* now you are wary. And so you should be.'

He hauled air into his lungs. Almost there. Any second now she would be gone from him. For ever. To take her rightful place.

* * *

Claudia trembled at the deluge of formidable power emanating from his frame as he paced the room, tormented by demons. Then he froze, closed his eyes as if reliving his darkest moments, and when they opened once more the pain she saw there was like a physical punch to her midriff, hurling her across the room.

'She reminds me that for the rest of my days I will pay for killing my own mother.'

Her stomach flinched so hard her gasp rent the air. She blinked wide, shell-shocked eyes. '*What?* No,' she said, shaking her head vigorously. 'No. You couldn't. I don't believe you.'

'I failed her,' he said, his eyes clouded, almost black. 'When I should have been protecting her. I am responsible for her brutal, agonising death.'

Some unseen hand gripped her heart and tore it from her chest. 'Your mother was…?' She couldn't say what was too horrific even to contemplate.

Lucas thrust his hands through his hair, twisted his fingers, punishing. 'Murdered,' he said, voice dark, haunted. 'I was working. We had no money, no food. So damn poor. He came for her when I should've been home, protecting her. Keeping her safe. *Dios,* I knew what he was capable of.'

He clenched his fists so hard she could see the dense muscle in his arms bunch and flex as if readying for a fight.

'Always I returned by nightfall, but that night I was careless. Missed my lift. Had to walk. Was too late. She was already broken. Her body twisted. Limp. Yet still she drew breath. And I stood, frozen. Weak.' His lips twisted with self-disgust. 'Did nothing to stop him walking free.'

She filled in the rest. It was oh-so-heart-shatteringly easy. He'd felt fear. For his mother. For himself.

'A coward,' he said, deathly quiet.

Oh, God. A sob threatened to tear from her throat as hot liquid splashed behind her eyes. Just in time she managed to swallow it whole. 'Don't you *dare* say such a thing. You told me you were young when your mother died.'

'*Sì*. I was fourteen. A man.'

'No, Lucas,' she said, her heart breaking in two. For him. 'A boy on the cusp of becoming a man.'

Such an emotionally tumultuous age, she knew. To lose his mother in such a way…

'No,' he growled, slashing an unsteady hand through the air. 'Do *not* look at me with pity. I don't deserve it. *Comprende?*'

Claudia nodded, schooled her features, determined to be strong—to be the woman he needed. Because she knew all about unwanted empathy. It would make him angrier still. 'Tell me what happened…to your mother. Please.' God, how she wanted to hold him. Comfort him. But she didn't have a hope of penetrating the dark forcefield shrouding him as he paced the floor. 'You knew the man who killed her?'

He stopped dead, no more than five feet in front of her, and sank his dark fierce gaze into her eyes. 'Of course I knew him, Claudia. He was my father.'

She tried—she really tried to keep still, to show nothing, but he must have seen the colour leach from her face. She could feel cold seeping through her body after all. *I knew what he was capable of...* 'Did he…?' She couldn't even say it. *Did he hurt you?* And no matter how hard she tried to stem the images they seemed to whip her mind, one after another.

His mouth twisted into a cruel sneer. 'Yes, Claudia, my father was the worst kind of man. He gambled every cent. Whored all over town. Drank himself into furious rages and beat her so badly she suffered severe internal haemorrhaging. Bled for hours before my very eyes.'

She drew her lips into her mouth, bit down hard, hauling every ounce of strength she could find to stop from crumpling to the floor. He had to live with his memories every hour of every day, and she felt damn pathetic for thinking *she'd* had a grim childhood. In comparison her life had been a bed of orange blossom.

She swallowed around the tight searing burn in her throat. 'I'm so sorry, Lucas. Truly.'

Claudia watched him slump into the deep sofa, bury his face in his hands. 'By the time I managed to get help, get her to the hospital, it was too late. I just sat there and watched her die. Powerless.' He spread his hands wide in front of him, looked down at his palms as if he was back there, in that very room. 'Blood dripped from my fingers. Pooled upon the floor. The longest six hours of my life.'

She scrambled onto her knees, then her feet. Wrapped the blanket around her body sarong-style and took a tentative step towards him, asking, begging. 'Let me hold you. Can I hold you? Please.'

'No!' he said, snapping upright, warding her off with one flat palm, eyes wild as pain howled through him. 'You stay away from me. I do not know what I'm capable of right now.'

Claudia slid back. Not because she was scared—no, she would never fear him—but because *he* was terrified. Terrified of the emotions pummelling through him. She wondered then if emotion reminded him of pain. Of weakness.

'I made a promise to her that day. That I would avenge her death.' His voice grew harder, darker, menacing. 'And I grew bigger, stronger—went after him. Ensured he was thrown into the worst hellhole on earth, where he died a befitting death. But that wasn't enough. Nowhere near enough. I went after every other murdering son of a bitch he was associated with. Hauled them one after another in front of every court in the land.'

'A vigilante.' *Of course.* She'd seen that roguish side to him from the start. The ruthless determination he radiated. The fierce power that held her in thrall. 'A hero.'

One corner of his mouth lifted in a satirical smirk. 'You think that, *querida,* if it keeps you warm at night.'

A blast of outrage stung her cheeks. 'I won't think it. I *know* it,' she said, her voice cracking as she thumped her heart with her fist. 'In here. Arunthia wouldn't be the country it is today without you. The people worship you. So don't you dare question your self-worth to me.'

He huffed a mirthless laugh. 'And right there,' he said, 'is the irony.'

'What do you mean?' she said, hating the cynicism, the disbelief in his eyes.

'Your father persuaded me to join the Arunthian Military. Taught me how to use power and strength for good, how to strive for honour by doing my duty to king and country. He saved my youthful dark soul. So when I came for you I had given him my word to protect you. And how do I repay him?' His lips twisted in self-disgust. 'I take your innocence. I ruin your reputation. I dishonour you and myself. Now I pay the price.'

The *price?*

'Oh, now, wait just a damn minute,' she said, her voice tremulous, her hand beseeching. 'I asked you to make love to me. I gave freely. I wanted you so much.' Her voice shattered along with her heart. Suddenly she didn't care what the admission would cost her, because he needed to hear it. 'Only you. It was never just sex for me, Lucas. I only wanted you. What's more, there was nothing, *nothing* dishonourable about what happened between us.'

Face contorting, he shook his head as if he fought an inner battle—his conscience warring with her words.

Then he flung his arms wide. '*Dios,* what is wrong with you, Claudia? Where is the hate?'

'In you, *cariño.* Never in me!' What was he thinking in that tormented mind? Realisation struck her down and she crumpled to the bed of pillows. Shook her head wildly. 'You could never, *ever* turn me away from you. Ever, *cariño.*'

His eyes flared with either anger or panic. She couldn't be sure. '*Dios,* do not call me that, Claudia.'

'Don't call you what…my darling?' Her voice turned hard, because she was so damn angry with him. 'Why? Because you don't deserve affection of the heart? You deserve it more than anyone, Lucas. Or is it because you intend to pay for the tragedy of your mother's death for eternity? Well, I say you've spent your whole life atoning for the past, and now it's your turn for some happiness.'

Eyes still haunted, he merely blinked up at her, as if horrified at the very thought. Either it had never occurred to him that she would forgive him or— *Oh, God.* Pain ripped through her. She'd been so sure something had changed during the night. She was scared, she realised, of his answer. But if this man had taught her anything it was courage.

'Or is it me?' she asked, wincing inwardly at the quiver in her voice. She cleared her throat, made it stronger. 'Am I not enough for you to try? Was it truly just sex for you?'

His jaw clenched, together with every muscle in his body, fiercely hard, resolute, and her stomach plunged to the floor.

'I warned you, did I not? I have sex. I walk away. I'm not a man to become attached to.'

Oh, it was far too late for that. Self-reliant Claudia had done the one thing she'd sworn she'd never do. She'd got close. And now just the thought of never seeing him again was like a huge gaping hole inside her—one that panged straight through her soul.

'You're right. You did warn me,' she said, trying for light, airy, scrambling for the cool, calm composure that had shielded her for so many years. She took a deep breath, trying to wrap her foggy mind around forming words. 'It's probably for the best. After all, a continent divides us in our desire to work, to atone, to give back. In that way we are similar, you and I.'

She tried for a smile but it felt brittle, edgy. Because she was about to lie outright. To relieve some of the strain marring his beautiful face and, though it pained her to admit it, she was still just a woman underneath. Pride she knew was a rare, fragile thing.

'Just as well I hadn't fallen for you.'

'Good—that is good,' he said, voice gruff, eyes drifting away from her. 'I have asked Armande to take you to the palace at noon. I have business in Barcelona, but I'll return for the ball.' Then he swung away to look out on the swirling mass of storm blowing in from the east. 'Tonight we keep it professional. You will stand in front of the nation and do your duty.'

She would have laughed if knives had not been tearing her apart. He thought of nothing, focused on nothing, but his duty to Arunthia. And wasn't that the story of her life?

Reaching for the anger, the hurt, she snatched at thin air. Because through it all she understood the rules he lived by. The horrific loss of his mother and his guilt dominated his every waking moment, and he found the honour he desperately needed by doing his job and fighting for the greater good. Just as Claudia had pledged her life to cure, to ease pain. She could never give that up, just as he couldn't.

All his rules made him the beautiful, strong, heroic man he was.

'Yes, Lucas. I'll do my duty. For *you*. On one condition.'

Lucas braced his arms against the plate glass as he stared into the turbulent froth of the ocean. Despite her words he knew she wished to see him again, and something close to need, yearning, clawed down his chest, lacerating his resolve.

Temptation was an ebb and flow of words in his mind. *Yes, I will come and see you, querido, hold you in my arms. I will try and give you everything you desire.*

Palms flat, he pushed off the window and turned to face her, guts twisting, his head in the midst of an almighty war…and his gaze crashed into the woman he'd failed. A woman sheltering a child from the storm, in pain, so much pain.

Claudia was wrong. He didn't deserve to be released from the shackles of blame.

Dios, how could he even think of allowing himself a relationship with Claudia? She made him feel every single emotion, and he knew the dangers of that. Loss of thought, of reason, control.

To this day he was plagued by his mother's death. What if

he had acted quicker, stopped the blood somehow, run faster for help? But he'd been afraid—yes, afraid—a destructive emotion that made you sloppy, careless, because love was so powerful it took away everything.

If he failed to protect her… *Dios,* just the thought made his blood run black. She was too precious.

Head high, the fawn cashmere blanket wrapped around her decadent curves, she walked towards him. Lucas stiffened, balling his fists to stop himself from reaching, from taking her one last time. To pacify the craving. Numb the pain. Because he refused to use her heavenly body in such a way.

Her step faltered and she sank her teeth into her lip. 'Did you hear me, Lucas?'

Like a potent aphrodisiac, her scent, *their* scent, curled up his nose, blurring thought.

'Ah, of course.' He'd almost forgotten. About her duty. His mission. That in itself should have told him something. 'Tell me your condition, Princesa.'

CHAPTER FOURTEEN

'PROMISE ME YOU will let go of the past.'

A cacophony of voices floated through the open window. Bristles stroked her scalp and diamond pins slid through lofty curls, yet through it all Claudia stared unseeingly into the gilt-edged dressing table mirror before her. Remembering the dark haunted look on Lucas's face as nine simple words tossed him further into purgatory.

So strong was his need to do his duty and get her to the palace, he'd given her his oath to try, however much it pained him. For, truly, what was the point of hurting, of living with such pain, when the past couldn't be changed.

'Claudine.' Her mother's serene face popped into view beside her. 'Where are you, I wonder?'

Thinking about my lover. Claudia winced inwardly as her cheeks rouged in the mirror and feathers of unease dusted her nape. 'Oh, nowhere in particular.'

Her mother arched one perfectly plucked brow, wholly unconvinced, and Claudia almost smiled. She could read her mother now, especially when they were alone, making her realise that Queen Marysse wore a mask of her very own.

'Pass me another pin, then, dear.'

Claudia reached for another pin, chose a pearl, and passed it over her shoulder. 'Don't you have staff to do this? Surely you don't have time.'

'Nonsense. I will make time. How many days and nights of my life have I spent wishing I could be there for you?'

Claudia closed her eyes, knowing it was time she listened to her own advice and let go of the past.

'I didn't know you felt that way, Mother.'

Perhaps Lucas was right. On that fateful day her mother had been unthinking, not uncaring. And maybe her parents had handled her illness the only way they knew how. By acting. Not by becoming overwrought with emotion—like her mother had during the accident. Her safety and health had been paramount to them. She'd never felt loved, but her parents must have cared. She only had to think of what Lucas had gone through and every memory seemed to fade. Diminish, somehow.

'Let us start over—could we, Claudine?' Her mother's warm fingers curled over her shoulder, squeezed through her cotton wrap. 'I am opening the new children's wing next week and I was hoping you would come.'

Claudia looked up…saw warmth and hope in her mother's gaze. She could do her duty while she was here, couldn't she? There was really no need for the frisson of panic that they might expect more. 'I'd like that.'

'Good. I have asked Lucas to arrange the security.'

Oh, honestly, even the mention of his name gave her palpitations. 'You saw Lucas this morning?'

'Briefly. Your father was in talks with Philippe Carone, but Lucas seemed anxious to meet with him. Henri saw him, of course, before he flew to—'

'Barcelona,' Claudia murmured through the clattering in her head.

Why had Lucas gone to see her father so suddenly? And why did her stomach scream at the thought? And why was her mother watching her so closely? They'd done nothing wrong. *Everyone* had sex. Right?

'Yes,' her mother said slowly, as she slid alongside Claudia to choose another pin from the gold tray. 'His headquarters are there.'

Some sixth sense told Claudia she should quit while she was ahead, but now she'd started talking her tongue didn't want to stop. 'Headquarters for what?'

Her mother's brow creased, amber eyes snapping up to Claudia's. 'LGAS, of course.'

Suddenly grateful she was sitting down, Claudia's mouth worked. '*The* LGAS? Lucas *owns LGAS?* How on earth did I miss that?' She slumped back into the chair. 'High-end security, renowned, the best in the world.' Always protecting, she mused with a secret smile…which then slid off her face. 'Wait a minute—doesn't LGAS have an aerodynamic wing? I travelled in one of his jets!' The word *wealth* didn't even begin to describe his inordinate success. God, she was so proud of him her heart ached.

'Of course you did, darling. Everyone important does.' Her mother heaved a theatrical sigh. 'Shoulders straight, Claudine. A hump is most unattractive.'

Claudia bolted upright. 'I can't believe I didn't see it.' For heaven's sake—did she go around with her eyes shut? What else had she missed?

'Lucas is a very private man,' her mother continued, her tone taut, her eyes narrowed on Claudia's face. 'Something I'm acutely grateful for. You are entitled to a private life, Claudine, I stress *private*.'

Claudia's stomach plunged. Was she so obvious? Or was the fact she'd been his guest enough to arouse suspicion? She'd never thought of that, had she? No, she'd just been desperate to stay with him. Only him. Because he made her feel safe. But how had it looked from the outside looking in? He worked for her father. He—

'Nothing is going on, Mother.' Well, apart from sex, and she wasn't telling her *that*.

'I am glad to hear it. The stakes are high. Think of your reputation. His work.'

She couldn't give two stuffs about her reputation. Despite every loaded inference to the contrary, she was going back to London! And Lucas was staying here.

Heart crashing against her ribs, she flinched at a brisk rap upon the door and the strutting in of her mother's PA, carrying a crushed velvet gift box.

Her mother passed the box to Claudia with a warning look. 'I will leave you now. Your father will be here on the hour.'

Waiting for the door to close, she felt a heady concoction of panic and excitement surge through her veins. At the click of the door she fumbled with the lid, tossed it to the floor and tore through layer upon layer of black tissue paper. Then time stood still as her eyes devoured the contents, her heart leaping up her throat.

'Oh, Lucas.'

Hand trembling, she picked up the thick cream-coloured card, ran her thumb over the strong, black masculine scroll. Laying the card upon the mirrored plate, just so, she returned to the box and lifted a pair of long pale gold gloves—exactly the same satin as the dress he'd known she was desperate to wear. The sheath, thank heavens, hung on the rack in front of her: a temptation she'd been unable to shake.

Twisting her hand this way and that, she saw small diamond studs wink at her from where they trailed up the full length of the cuff in a perfect row.

Tears glistened behind her eyes.

This from the man who professed he didn't feel. Oh, but she knew he *could* feel—every emotion, ten-fold. The power of which scared him to death.

Lucas cared for her. He must. Was he lending her his strength? God, how she ached for his touch. A touch she couldn't allow herself to hope for, because she was beginning to realise she'd put his position at risk. The honourable duty he lived for.

Dressing, she imagined him sprawled across the sofa, watching her, dark hunger glittering in his sapphire eyes as she smoothed sheer ivory silk stockings up her legs. Legs he'd kissed every inch of. Tying the ribbons on her corset, it was as if his fingers curled around the supple silk, pulling her, cinching her tight.

This from the man whose written words echoed in her head as she stood at the top of the opulent sweeping staircase holding onto her father's arm, her heart a thump, thump, thumping beat.

Hold your head high, Princesa.

Claudia lifted her chin. Opened her eyes on a monstrously titanic room where every sinister eye looked upon her.

Be proud of the woman you have become.

She took one step, then another, begging her feet not to fail her now. Down, down, down she went, gliding into the palatial, softly lit ballroom. The crowd hushed, her mind locked on Lucas…the satin caressed her wrists like a lover's healing kiss.

This from the man whose eyes sought hers as soon as her feet hit the polished floor with a look of such intense pride she had to grip her father's arm not to fall.

Her heart filled, gushed, overflowed.

This from the man she'd fallen deeply and irrevocably in love with.

This from the man she now had to protect.

Lucas stood in the midst of inane chatter, searching for the satisfaction of a mission accomplished. It was like digging for mines in the dark.

Statuesque, sanguine, Princess Claudine Verbault had finally taken her rightful place. The sight of which Lucas knew was his cue to leave. Yet his designer-clad feet were as if suctioned to the silver-toned marble as he hauled air into his tight lungs, clenched every hard muscle in his body until his bones ached.

That he'd lasted one hour and thirty-three minutes without manhandling her out of the room was a miracle in itself. And what the *hell* was Henri doing, throwing Philippe Carone at her every chance he got? The business magnate just happened to be one of the most eligible bachelors in Europe. And if the sleaze-bag danced with Claudia one more time—if he looked at Claudia one more time, stripping the tight sheath from her body with his marauding eyes—Lucas would launch the man across the room.

Thrusting his fingers to his throat, he yanked at the stiff collar.

Madre de Dios, surely Henri was not contemplating such a match? After everything she'd been through? Hadn't she paid enough of a price to Arunthia? To lose her parents, her home, while so tender and vulnerable.

Lucas closed his eyes, took a deep breath, infusing his brain with some sense. No, he was wrong, Henri wouldn't ask such a thing of her.

But *Dios—Carone*? The man wasn't much taller than she was. How could he possibly protect her? Lucas could do a better job with his eyes shut! What the hell had *ever* made him think otherwise? No longer was he fourteen years old. No longer did he doubt his own strength. Claudia had trusted him with her life—curled her naked body into his. Even after he'd told her the truth of his past she'd cared not. Still she'd trusted implicitly. Still she had wanted to be held. And he'd walked away. Focused on duty. Rammed her responsibilities down her pretty throat. And if Henri were serious about Carone she would be strangled by duty until the day she died. Lucas had never considered happiness important. Until her. Until now.

On the far side of the room he saw Carone set his sights and begin walking towards her.

Excusing himself from the cluster of foreign dignitaries, Lucas swerved through the crowd, eyes locked on Claudia, his arms begging to pick her up, take her away. If he didn't feel so damn sick he would laugh at the irony.

She turned, as if sensing him, eyes filling with an instant of warmth before veiling, cooling—a look he did not care for.

'Good evening, Your Royal Highness,' he said, with a formal nod. 'You look exquisite.'

'Thank you, Lucas, you don't look too bad yourself.' She forced a smile and his stomach hollowed…then shot to the floor when Carone sidled up beside her and Claudia offered the other man a sincere warm slide of her lips.

'This dance is *mine,* Carone,' he growled. 'Excuse us.'

Lucas slid a protective hand over the base of Claudia's spine, curled his fingers up around her waist and felt her muscles stiffen beneath his touch. He thrust away the sliver of panic; he'd wanted professional and now he was getting it.

'I have a better idea,' he said, tightening his fingers as they walked towards the dance floor—and took a swift unheeded side-step through the double doors leading on to the terrace beyond and the privacy of a star-studded sky. The chilly nip of the air did a miserable job of lowering his temperature.

'Are you sure this is such a good idea?' she asked, quickly sliding from his hold.

The loss of contact did abominable things to his mind-set. Lucas closed the doors, drowning out the noise with a satisfying click, and swivelled back to face her, taking a good swift kick to the guts as he drank her in.

All glamorous sophistication, she stood by the wrought-iron railings, pearly teeth gnawing at her rouged lip, top-to-toe in gold satin which hugged and caressed every voluptuous curve. His palms itched to indulge. Stroke. Cosset. *Dios,* would the craving ever cease?

He balled his hands. 'Claudia…' he managed, before wondering what the hell to say.

The lines of strain eased from her brow as her mouth tilted knowingly. 'Thank you for the gift.'

'You're very welcome,' he said, still loath to admit, even to himself, why he'd sent it. So she would feel his possessive touch around her beautiful wrists. A touch she'd discarded within minutes. 'You didn't seem to need them for too long.' Which was a good thing, he assured himself, ignoring the twinge in his chest.

'Ah, well,' she said, her cheeks pinkening to rose-gold, 'I'd quite forgotten how slippery satin was.'

Lucas swallowed hard. *Dios,* he was dying here.

Dying? No, it was worse than that. He felt as if he was about to lose the most important thing in his world. Again.

'So slippery,' she continued, probably in an effort to keep things light, oblivious to the dark storm raging inside of him, 'that after thirty minutes the caterers were three champagne flutes down and in all conscience I thought I better take them off.'

The tension in his midsection evaporated on a laugh. One side of her lush mouth curved and his arms ached to pick her up, carry her away.

Chin dipping, she peeked up at him through dense sooty lashes. 'I found out something else tonight. Or should I say *realised* something else. *You* gave me the money. The funding. My parents would never have offered. How it must have pained you to coerce me.'

He shrugged. Made it lazy. He would have given her one hundred million. 'I do not regret it.' How could he when he never would have tasted heaven otherwise? 'So do not forgive me,' he bit out.

'Oh, I will—and I do,' she said softly, her eyes now full—the first signs of a thaw?—brimming with a warmth that made his skin prickle, his heart thud. 'I'm in awe of you, Lucas. To come so far against all the odds.' She reached up, trailed one finger down his jaw. 'I'm so proud of the man you have become.'

Dios, he'd had it with this senseless woman.

Snap went his resolve, his strength. One step forward and he reached out…and every muscle in his arms, every vein in his body, froze as her lashes fluttered closed and she shook her head.

'I should go back inside,' she murmured. 'Thank you for everything.'

His head jerked. Thank you? For what…? *The sex*? Was *that* why she'd wanted him to come to London…for more *sex*? Something told him he'd slipped into the irrationality danger zone here, but *Madre de Dios—thank you*? As if she could just walk away and forget.

Like hell she would.

Ignoring the pop of her eyes, Lucas dug his hand into the hair at her nape, yanked her head back and flung his mouth against hers. He muffled her shock with his lips and kissed her irrational mouth while a noxious tangle of emotions knotted his guts. Plundering her mouth with his tongue, he curved his hands around the delicate span of her waist and crushed her against him.

A fist of anxiety clenched his heart when she stiffened… but then she wrapped her arms about his shoulders, thrust her fingers in his hair and tugged, giving as good as she got. The flush of relief turned to liquid fire as she blazed in his arms.

The crackle and hum of static energy surged between their bodies, bouncing from one point of contact to the other. *Dios,* they created enough electricity to power the eastern grid. He couldn't let her go. He needed…

A flash lit the sky. Then another. A slam. A door? Fireworks?

A gasp rent the air. Not his. Not hers.

Lips froze, still close, and Lucas could taste her panting breath as it whispered across his tongue.

Thuds hit his temples as reality cracked through his skull, his entire body vibrating with the force of it.

Hands falling from her pale, horrified face, Lucas took a step back, closed his eyes. No, no, *no! Dios,* her reputation would be in tatters.

Plink. Plink. One light after another lit the sky. Cameras. *Dios,* she hated cameras. She would run, he knew. Hide.

Hands fisting into a violent clench, his eyes flew open. And locked onto her amber fire.

Still here. Still standing tall. Regal. Brave. Courageous. After everything she'd been through he could not, *would not* walk away from her now.

Dark waves of fury poured from his rigid shoulders while an earthquake shook the paving beneath her feet.

Oh, God, why had she kissed him back? She was supposed to be staying away from him!

Her mother's voice came to her. *Think of your reputation... his work.* And the cold night began to seep through her skin, burrow into her stomach.

'Tell me this isn't happening,' she whispered.

'Consequences,' he said, his voice dark, fierce, harder than ever before. 'Now we face them.'

'Oh, Lucas, I'm so sorry.'

His words screamed in her head. *Your selfishness is astounding.* In all the years she'd loathed her own reflection she'd never envisaged disliking the person she was inside. Had she once given thought to the impact on Lucas should they ever be found out? No. She'd just wanted him. So desperately. Unseeing of the consequences.

Swarms of black locusts poured onto the patio—one brawny security man for every ravenous tabloid fiend.

'Tell me now,' he said, his eyes swirling with a turbulent storm. 'What do you want, Claudia?'

She wanted to fix it. Put everything right. Make good on the destruction she'd caused. The alternative didn't bear thinking about. But she *did* think about it. Because her brain wouldn't switch off. Would Lucas the Honourable propose? Be trapped *by her* for eternity? Or, worse still, would her father discharge him? Strip him of his honour?

Never.

Claudia could fix this. Make sure he kept his job. His life. Everything that made him the man he was. The man she loved. And she knew exactly how to do it.

'I will fight for you,' he avowed. 'Tell me what you want.'

Her throat stung. Still he would fight for her. Her brave knight. But even knights answered to their king.

'To be free. To go home. That's all I've ever wanted.' *Until you. Only you. God,* her heart was breaking.

His jaw hard, the shutters slammed down over his face. 'Very well.'

He took a step back and beckoned to Armande with a flick of his fingers, told him to corral all the reporters out front for Lucas to deal with.

Claudia inhaled his scent one last time as she snuck around him, raised her chin and strode towards her father.

She ignored the disappointment weighing heavy in his eyes. She'd make him happy soon enough.

'Can I speak with you, Father?'

'My office. Twenty minutes.'

Claudia spent the longest, most agonising twenty minutes of her life pacing the living room in the private quarters of the Palace. The silvery moon cast eerie shadows over the oppressive grandeur, making her shiver. But this way, *sans* artificial light, she could keep one eye on the grandfather clock and sneak a peek at Lucas out front, his huge body looming over a member of the paparazzi.

Thankfully they'd only had a small audience on the terrace but…God, the look on his face as they'd parted ways. She would never forget it. Fierce, yet strangely bleak. He must hate her for placing him in this position.

A loud gong echoed off the oak-panelled walls like a death-knell and she stiffened her backbone, swept through the room, down the cavernous hallway to her father's office. Palm flat, she pushed through the door, turned, closed it with a soft click and spun around to face him—sitting behind his wide desk in a high-backed brown leather chair, focusing his flinty gaze on her face.

'Claudine.'

'Father.' She strode towards his desk to stand opposite him

and lifted her chin. 'I have a proposition for you.' Even as she hoped to reach a compromise—something she should have considered well before now—she realised that on the back of ruining the Anniversary Ball her timing sucked.

'Let's hear it,' he said, barely suppressed temper firing his cheeks.

She kept her cool. Reached for her mask. Because she'd never needed it more.

'I apologise for any embarrassment I've caused you tonight. Truly. But the fault is mine and I'm quite willing to make it up to you.' Her voice almost cracked on the last, and she bit her inner cheek to stop from crying out, pleading with him.

'Unless you are willing to come home for good, I do *not* want to hear it.'

She tried to swallow but it was impossible. So much for compromise.

How right Lucas had been. *You cannot change who you are, Princesa.* And hadn't she suspected all along that the moment she stepped foot on Arunthian soil her freedom would be lost?

Brittle was surely the only word to describe her smile. 'All right, Father. I'll come home.'

His clipped grey brows hiked just a touch. 'You will give up your work?' he said, still disbelieving.

The lump in her chest caught fire and tore up her throat. Years of research…the children she'd left behind…Bailey. *Forgive me. I'll make it up to you. I swear it.* 'Yes.'

She would never have believed it possible of her autocratic father, but his head actually jerked. Strange how that small reaction pleased her—until she beheld the gleam in his eyes.

'Will you marry Carone?'

Whack—the first crack in her armour ripped through her stomach and she stiffened to prevent the flinch. She should have known there was some reason he'd been throwing Carone at her. She couldn't contemplate what such an allegiance would involve or she'd throw up on her father's pristine desk. Didn't royals marry for love these days? Then again, what did it matter when she couldn't have the man she loved? And if she lived elsewhere she wouldn't have to see him every day. She could forget. *Impossible.*

The effort to stand tall while her heart was bleeding made her legs throb. 'Yes,' she said, proud of the steel in her voice. 'As long as you do something for me.'

That cool, flinty gaze narrowed imperceptibly. 'I am intrigued to know what would make you give up so much, Claudine.'

'Lucas gets to keep his job, his honour, and to do his duty for Arunthia. You need him, Father, I know you do. And he… he needs it too.' She wondered then if the virtual stranger before her could hear the love in her voice. So she licked her dry lips and focused on the aspect that would carry more weight with this ruler of a nation. 'The people love him. He's their hero.' *And mine too.*

Her father nodded slowly, his bushy brows low over his eyes. 'I see.'

The stern lines of his face softened, to make him appear younger somehow. She blinked hard, wondering if the transformation was a mirage.

'Does Lucas know how you feel about him?'

A breath she'd had no idea she was holding whooshed out of her and her head bowed—her mask slipping to shatter upon the floor. 'God, I hope not.'

'Too. Late.'

Slam went her hand to her heart as those two little words delivered in that deadly fierce voice echoed around the room.

Slowly she turned. *Oh, no.* 'Lucas.'

Sprawling insolently, he encompassed one huge black wing chair, the tie of his tux loose around his neck, one devilish dark brow raised. And she'd swear she could hear his molars crack.

'Big mistake, *querida*.'

CHAPTER FIFTEEN

HAVING JUST SPENT the last forty minutes in the depths of hell, Lucas wasn't feeling so good.

'Excuse us, Henri.'

'Of course, my friend.' He heard the smile in Henri's voice, ignored it. God only knew what the man was thinking after Lucas had played every strategic manoeuvre to get Claudia back to bloody London!

Dios, he was going to make her pay.

Wide-eyed, still shaking like a blade of grass on a breeze, Claudia stood, her gaze flicking from Lucas to her father, back to Lucas.

Still she was unsure who held the power—over him, over her. He had no idea what had happened to make her doubt his dominant strength, but soon she would remember Lucas was his own man with his own damn rules. A fact Henri had always accepted.

'We leave. Now,' he said. Toxic nausea churned inside him, poisoning his voice.

Palm flat to the base of her spine, he gave her a deft push out through the door, down the hallway to the front of the private wing, farther still into the night.

'You're angry with me?' she asked, her voice small, quivery, as she lifted the skirts of her dress and negotiated the stone steps.

'Of course not. Whatever made you think such a thing?'

He jabbed at the open door, being held open by Armande, his voice petrifying the wildlife. 'Get in the damn car.'

Armande bowed his head shortly before they both slid into the stifling interior.

'It must have been Armande,' she murmured, plastering herself against the opposite end of the cream leather bench and nipping her plump bottom lip.

Dios, more enclosed spaces! He rammed his fingers down the inside of his shirt and tore another button free as the car meandered down the tree-lined incline.

'I thought it was you with the reporters outside.'

'Clearly.' Although he'd never been more grateful for *not* being somewhere in his entire life. To think she might have left!

He scrubbed his hands over his face, his hair. Checked the privacy screen. Unable to wait a second longer to vent all over her.

'I asked you on the terrace,' he said, hearing the dark blend of incredulity and anger in his own voice, 'what you wanted. That was a *very* simple question, Claudia!'

She winced, reached up, rubbed her brow. 'I know you did.'

'And what did you say to me? That you wanted to be *free!*' He balled his fists on his thighs as his volume soared. 'Yet now you will marry that sleaze *Carone?*'

'Well, I—'

'Dios, Claudia, I had a goddamn coronary right there in the room!' He laid a hand on his chest to check his heart was still there. Still beating. Like a pneumatic drill.

'You did?' she asked, turning to look at him, her brow pinched. 'Well, I was just trying to think of a way to fix things.'

'Do me a favour, *querida?* Do not over-think. It scares the hell out of me.' He could barely breathe just thinking about it. The way she had stood there—so calm, a stranger to him— telling Henri she would marry that tiny fool *before* she'd bothered to stipulate why. Drawing out his pain as if he was lying on some medieval rack in the dungeon.

And then there she was, his little warrior, no longer fighting for herself but fighting for him. And, *Dios,* still he could barely breathe.

Pursing her lips, she crossed her arms tight over her chest. Her lush breasts eased out of the ruched bands of her bodice and he had to tear his eyes away before he hauled her into his lap. Three minutes and they would be home. Surely he could wait that long?

Yet he could feel her skin start to bristle. She was thinking again. *Damn.*

'You both sat there, no doubt having sealed my fate, and let me say all that stuff!'

What was she? Embarrassed? 'Let me assure you there was no pleasure to be gained.' From the first part at least. And he would have made his presence known if her words had not struck him dumb.

'And how is it going to look now?' she said, her fiery temper bubbling to the surface. 'There were still some reporters milling around back there.'

Lucas snapped. 'To hell with the paparazzi! I do not care for other men's opinions. And you'd better get used to the attention, *querida.* I imagine once news of our engagement hits your face will cover every rag in the western hemisphere!'

Her small hand curled around the base of her throat. '*Engagement?* Oh, God, I should've known. What did he say? What have you done?'

He had done nothing bar fight for her freedom! But he wasn't done with punishing her yet.

'Did I not tell you that *I* make the rules, Claudia? And I assure you, your fate was sealed well before tonight, *cariña.*' Although, to be fair, for an intelligent man it had taken him a while.

'What's that supposed to mean?'

Lucas rocked forward as the car pulled to a stop and within twenty seconds he had her ensconced in the house. His house. Their house. Their living room.

Claudia stood in the middle of the floor, feet shifting, watching him warily. 'All my things are at the palace.'

'I will send for them tomorrow,' he said, tearing his jacket from his torso. 'You will stay here. With me. Always.'

'Lucas will you stop this? I haven't agreed to anything and I refuse to trap you!'

Grabbing fistfuls of his shirt, he ripped it from his body. Buttons pinged off every surface as he tore it off, tossed it to the floor. Then he swung back to face her, pointed at the gold sheath. 'Take it off.'

Her lips parted on an indrawn breath and she flushed crimson from head to foot. 'The *dress?* Why?'

'Because *his* fingerprints are all over it,' he ground out. 'And because I have just been through the worst forty minutes of my adult life and I need to *hold* you!'

'Oh.' Pursing her lips, she reached for the zip at her side and slowly pulled the metal pin down, inch by excruciating inch. His pulse spiked as the contaminated gold satin slinked from her luscious curves to pool on the floor at her feet, leaving her standing in…

'Madre de Dios.'

'You recognise it?' she asked, voice husky, sexy as hell.

Tight ivory cinched her small waist, widened at her full spilling breasts. Lace-top silk stockings and crystal-studded gold heels completed the evocative feast.

Lucas scrubbed his palm over his heart. Just to check again. 'The lingerie boutique. In town.'

'Ah. So I *did* have your full attention?'

'Always, *querida,*' he said, shucking off his trousers and shoes until he stood in snug black hipsters, never taking his eyes from those glorious centrefold curves. Curves he now gripped at the waist and hauled to straddle him as he plunged to the sofa.

Wrapping his arms around her, he buried his face in the soft skin at her neck and inhaled, over and over, rubbing his lips against her delicate collarbone, trying to pull her tighter into him.

She made that erotic purring noise that drove him *loco*.

'Agony,' she whispered. 'At least we're good at this, I suppose.'

'Stop it. You are thinking again.'

'Can't help it.'

'I know,' he said, pulling back to kiss the curve of her neck, the sexy dip behind her ear. 'That brain of yours was one of the first things that hit me. *Dios,* one look at you and it was like crashing headlong into a solid brick wall. Then every touch was like flirting with a minefield. Every look was a bullet between my eyes. And when you spoke those words tonight…'

He loosened his hold, just enough to sit back, cup her face and sink into her amber fire. 'So brave. My beautiful brave Princesa. I have never felt more proud or more love for you.'

Her long black sooty lashes fluttered while her delicate jaw went slack. *'Really?'*

'Claudia, Claudia. The night I took you I made a choice. I chose *you*. Not duty, not Arunthia. You. I knew then, *cariña*. One taste and I would lose it all. I knew then I would resign. And I would do it all over again in a heartbeat just to hold you.'

Moisture pooled in her eyes and his stomach twisted as one dewy droplet trickled down her face and slid over his thumb.

'You resigned?' she said in a teary whisper.

'Sí. I resigned this morning. I would've done so days ago, but I couldn't leave you long enough. Tonight was my final duty.'

'But you said…you told me there could never be anything more. I thought you would never open your heart to me.'

'It took me a while to realise you were already there. I could not get my head around deserving you. So long I have lived with the guilt. But then you told me you were proud of the man I have become. And if *you* thought I was worthy who was I to argue?' He shrugged, tried to make it lazy, still not entirely convinced, but…

'Guilt? I wanted to die when I realised I'd cost you everything. Have you ever thought for one moment that I don't deserve you?'

'No,' he said fiercely. 'And do not let me hear you say such a thing again.'

'Yes, Lucas,' she said, a mocking smile teasing her lips.

He growled. 'It scared the hell out of me that I might fail to protect you. But then I thought how could I possibly trust anyone else? It is impossible. Only me.'

'Only you.' She trailed her fingertips down the side of his face and he nuzzled into her touch. 'Although maybe if you eased off a bit…? I can paddle in the sea without disaster striking.'

He growled again—deeper, harder. That was the only answer she was getting right now. The roll of her eyes told him she knew it.

'But still I held out,' he said. 'Until I heard the words you spoke to your father. Filled with such bravery. And there was I—a warrior shielding my heart, without the courage to love you. After everything you've been through you stood there, my little warrior, and gave up your work and your freedom for me. I was humbled by you, *querida.*'

She reached up, softly brushed his hair from his temple. 'I'd do anything for you. I love you so much.'

Lucas closed his eyes. That was it. She'd said it. She was his. Always.

Claudia nestled impossibly closer, peppering kisses all over his gorgeous face. He'd chosen her and it was as if the Philharmonic Orchestra was playing in her soul, making her blood sing, her body hum in ecstasy—alive, so vibrantly alive.

And because she knew he needed to hear it Claudia said the words, over and over, as she kissed his warm lips. 'I love you, Lucas, only you.' She added that last bit because the insane man was jealous beyond belief and, knowing he felt every emotion ten-fold, he must be in serious torment.

His hands slipped from her face and he began to pull the pins from her hair. 'I want it down around your shoulders. Over me. And, *Dios,* I'll have to leave you and go back to your father in the morning. It is a question of honour.'

'Wait a minute… You mean you didn't ask him already? Well, what on earth were you talking about in there?'

'Getting you back to London,' he ground out. 'Like you asked!'

'Oh.' An inappropriate laugh burst past her lips. God, they made a sorry pair. Mind you, she couldn't regret a minute—not whilst in the midst of this heavenly pay-off. 'So why are we getting married?' It was obvious, but she couldn't resist.

'Because I damn well say so!'

Oh, he was so fantastically fierce. She had a huge grin on her face, she knew. 'You love me?'

'*Sí.* Desperately.'

'We're going to get married?'

'*Sí.* I can wait one week for you to arrange something.'

'One *week?*'

'Only one. My heart cannot take any more.' Her hair tumbled down around her shoulders and he groaned, thick and low. 'I will take you to visit Bailey and build you a new place for your work here. The best in the world.'

Claudia flung her arms around his neck, sank her fingers into his hair and breathed him in while her brain tripped. What else did she want? She was on a roll. She could have every little thing she'd secretly dreamed of.

She sprang back. 'Can we have a baby too?'

His throat convulsed. He went pale. Claudia's heart pinched, but she told herself not to be disappointed—it was only one little dream. She could push it back down.

'I never thought I deserved such a thing,' he said, wearing that haunted look that made her heart weep for him.

'Oh, Lucas, you deserve everything—and I'll spend my whole life proving it to you.'

One corner of his sexy mouth quirked. 'I want a baby girl with amber eyes and honey-gold skin.'

Typical, then, that she wanted a boy with rich sapphire blues. 'I don't think nature is going to listen to your rules, my darling.'

'Of course it will.'

She laughed. 'God, I love you.'

His hot gaze dropped to her chest. 'I love this thing you are wearing, but I want it off.'

'Pull the ribbons here,' she said, running her fingertip provocatively from the dip at the base of her throat to her cleavage, to rest on a line of tiny bows trailing down the front.

One after another he pulled the ties free—colour slashing his cheekbones as he unwrapped her. And if she'd thought he was hard beneath her already she'd been oh-so-very-wrong.

'Did you hear what I said about my dreams that day?' she asked, breathy as she undulated against him. Heat flooded her core, soaking her skimpy panties.

A husky groan poured from his mouth. 'I would not have a heard a freight train rolling through town, *cariña.* I was too busy imagining you in this sinful contraption.' The tight material gave way under the weight of her breasts, parting. 'My imagination was scarily accurate. *Dios,* Claudia, I need to be inside you.'

Lifting her arms, she peeled the corset from her body and let it fall to the floor.

His hot, heavy eyes raked over her flushed skin, his feverish hands following in their wake. He cupped one of her breasts, taking all the weight from her shoulder, and she leaned forward, needing the crush of his talented fingers.

'Tell me, *querida.* While I can still think.'

She licked her lips as he scraped his thumb over the tight peak, making her shudder.

'You said every princess dreams of Prince Charming. And I…I tried to tell you. I used to lie in bed and dream of one man.' Dreams…stories she'd passed onto Bailey. 'A warrior who would charge through the hospital walls…or in our case my lab. Sweep me off my feet. Save me from myself.'

She caught his questioning gaze, held it. 'I used to dream of being kissed by my hero. The Dark Knight.'

He grinned one of those gooey bad-boy smiles that made everything hot and wet, gripped the strip of lace around the top of her thighs and tore her panties clean off. 'I am adoring your dreams, *Just Claudia*.'

'Oh, I have tons more,' she said, sheathing him. Loving him.

He curled his hand around her nape, pulled her down to his mouth and murmured against her lips, 'And I shall make every one come true.'

Then he kissed her. Her hero. Her Dark Knight.

* * * * *

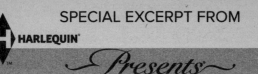

SPECIAL EXCERPT FROM

HARLEQUIN®

Presents

USA TODAY *bestselling author Lucy Monroe brings you
a passionate new duet,* BY HIS ROYAL DECREE,
from Harlequin® Presents®, starting with
ONE NIGHT HEIR *in July 2013.*

* * *

"I will not leave you again." It was a vow, accompanied by the slipping of the ring onto her finger.

Even though it was prompted by her pregnancy and the fact she now carried the heir to the Volyarus throne, the promise in his voice poured over the jagged edges of her heart with soothing warmth. The small weight of the metal band and diamonds on her finger was a source of more comfort than she would ever have believed possible.

She was not sure her heart would ever be whole again, but it did not have to hurt like it had for ten weeks.

"I won't leave you, either."

"I know." A small sound, almost a sigh, escaped his mouth. "Now we must convince your body that it still belongs to me."

"You have a very possessive side."

"This is nothing new."

"Actually, it kind of is." He'd shown indications of a possessive nature when they were dating, but he'd never been so primal about it before. "You're like a caveman."

His smile was predatory, his eyes burning with sensual intent. "You carry my child. It makes me feel *very* possessive, takes me back to the responses of my ancestors."

Air escaped her lungs in an unexpected whoosh. "Oh."

"I have read that some pregnant women desire sex more often than usual."

"I…" She wasn't sure what she felt in that department right now.

She always seemed to want him and could not imagine her hormones increasing that all too visceral need.

"However, I had not realized the pregnancy could impact the father in the same way." There was no mistaking his meaning.

Maks wanted her. And not in some casual, sex-as-physical-exercise way. The expression in his dark eyes said he wanted to devour her, the mother of his child, sexually.

Gillian shivered in response to that look.

"Cold?" he purred, pushing even closer. "Let me warm you."

"I'm not co—" But she wasn't allowed to finish the thought.

His mouth covered hers in a kiss that demanded full submission and reciprocation.

* * *

Find out what happens when this powerful prince raises the stakes of their marriage of convenience in ONE NIGHT HEIR, out July 2013!

And don't miss the explosive second story, PRINCE OF SECRETS, available August 2013.

REQUEST YOUR
FREE BOOKS!

2 FREE NOVELS PLUS
2 FREE GIFTS!